city of forgetting

ALSO BY ROBERT MAJZELS
Hellman's Scrapbook (Cormorant Books)

city
of
forgetting

A novel

Robert
Majzels

The Mercury Press

The publisher gratefully acknowledges the financial assistance of the Canada Council for
the Arts and the Ontario Arts Council.

Cover design by Gordon Robertson
Cover photograph by P. Elaine Sharpe
Map by Jim Roberts
Edited by Beverley Daurio
Copy edited by Jim Roberts
Page design, composition and film by Moveable Type Inc.
Printed and bound in Canada by Metropole Litho

A NOTE ON THE TYPE
Typeset using QuarkXPress in 11.35 point Bulmer, with heads in 17 point Village Bold.
Bulmer is a transitional face designed circa 1790 by William Martin for William Bulmer's
Shakespeare Press; Village was designed in 1932 by Frederic W. Goudy.

FIRST EDITION
  2 3 4 5 01 00 99

Canadian Cataloguing in Publication Data

Majzels, Robert, 1950 –
    City of forgetting

Includes bibliographical references.
ISBN 1-55128-045-0

I. Title.

PS8576.A525C57 1997   C813'.54   C97-931807-6
PR9199.3.M34C57 1997

Represented in Canada by the Literary Press Group
Distributed in Canada by General Distribution Services

THE MERCURY PRESS
2569 Dundas Street West, Toronto, Ontario M6P 1X7

Acknowledgements

This novel was written with the financial assistance of the Canada Council for the Arts and le ministère des Affaires culturelles du Québec.

My thanks also to Tewanhni'tátshon and Kanien'kéha Owén:na Otióhkwa (the Mohawk Language Curriculum Centre) for their assistance with the Mohawk language, to Maria Montejo and Patrice Giasson for the tango lessons, to Maria Eugenia Saul for her keen Spanish eye, to Gabriel Baugniet for teaching me how to beg in ancient Greek, and to Erin Mouré, Anne Dandurand and others for their careful reading and suggestions. I am profoundly grateful to Joe Kotler, who donated the priceless services of Moveable Type, and to the staff of that establishment, in particular Jim Roberts, for his intelligence and proofreading skills. Finally, thanks to Beverley Daurio for her generosity and commitment to contemporary writing.

The text which follows is traversed by the writings of Kate Chopin, Charles Baudelaire, Raymond Chandler, Gustave Flaubert, Le Corbusier, Leo Tolstoy, Charlotte Brontë, Karl Marx, Jean Rhys, William Shakespeare, Æschylus, Gertrude Stein, Ché Guevara, le Père Vimont, Federico García Lorca, Gabino Coria Peñaloza, The Mohawk Nation, Pablo Neruda, Bob Dylan, Mao Zedong, Julio Cortázar and others, among whom are many of which the author is not aware. For more detailed acknowledgements, see the notes at the end of the book.

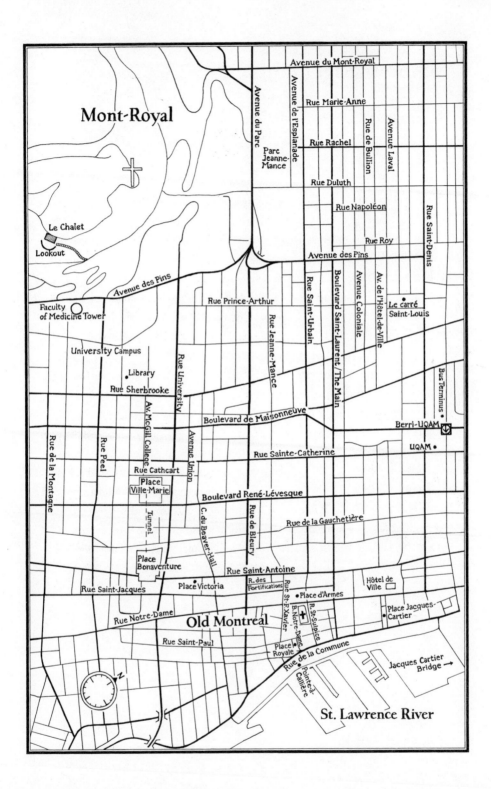

¡Qué esfuerzo del caballo
por ser perro!
    Federico García Lorca

ἆρ᾽ ἐστί σοι ὀβολὸς περισσός ;

Morning Ablutions

Almost dawn, lying on her back, her eyes opening to a pattern of yellow fish on a purple sea. For that initial fleeting instant she is free, empty of thought or memory or self. Then a weight across her legs shifts, and gritting her teeth against the pain of muscle and bone, she rolls onto her side. Return to the body. Her eyes focus and she sees the girl kneeling asleep at the foot of the hammock. The weight she felt in half-waking is the girl's arm flung across her calves. The weight that woke her. At the sight of the girl at her feet—the tight skin of the shaved head, the sharp thin bone at the top of the cranium stretching the pale, almost translucent scalp, the dark shadow of bristle just beginning to come to the surface, the three silver rings dangling from one nostril—immediately the thick glutinous fluid of memory rises to the surface and Clytæmnestra herself is reconstituted in her entirety, almost the identical person she was before falling asleep last night, but for the addition of her dreams.

Slowly, painstakingly, and without waking the girl, who would only insist on following her, she climbs down from her sleeping post, thrusts the knotted hair from her face and rearranges her ragged robes, which had tangled round her sleeping thighs. The signs of early spring are everywhere: the winter's snow pouring off the mountain, the bare-branched trees scribbled against a flat tin sky, the muddy ground, uneven and treacherous. She steps, barefoot, into the dark oozing soil, the cold grip of death pulling on her ankles. Forces her way toward the path, using her arms to ward off the razor ferns and stabbing branches. And pauses. Pauses on the rocky path to catch a few thin strands of breath before striding, head high, out of the forest and up to the summit.

To her right, on a crest facing the east: Mount Royal's cross, a Tatlinesque monument of steel girders outlined in electric white light and suspended in space above the city. She turns to her left, toward the wide stone-paved demilune of the lookout, ignoring, for the moment, the Chalet, a long high-roofed construction of dark wood and stone, housing a ceremonial hall, a hot-dog and ice-cream stand, and public facilities. Later she will go in and wash up, before the few off-season tourists arrive. But first she walks along the circumference of the battlements to the midway point of the semicircle. There, as she has done every dawn and every dusk for twenty-five hundred years, Clytæmnestra stands alone and scans the horizon.

The city, a dirty dishrag stretched out at her feet; the skyscrapers stacked up against the river; the trussed arch of the Jacques Cartier Bridge, as though the mountain crucifix had tipped over into the water. Briefly, a rain shower erupts, sweeps past her and across the river into the curving plain.

Clytæmnestra, daughter of Leda, whose beauty brought Zeus tumbling like a shot goose out of the heavens. Clytæmnestra, whose sister Helen's gaze turned the Aegean sea blood-red. Clytæmnestra, Queen of Argos, dark brilliant lover, last matriarch to rule the city, killer of kings, assassin of the patriarch. Clytæmnestra, great Agamemnon blazing in your nets and the poet kneeling at your feet to catch a phrase, a single word tumbling from the long curls of your ink-black hair. You stand, immobile, on the battlements, your skin crumbling ancient parchment, your breasts shrunken and dry, your once arching back a gnarled winter's branch.

Ah, but my hair still flows night-black to the water, and my eyes still pierce the fog above the city and across the sea. I can see, from torchlight to torchlight, from mountaintop to mountaintop, across the plains and straits to the burning fires within the very walls of Troy. Twenty-five centuries I have stood upon these ramparts. Waited and watched. Watched for an end to the war, for the return of my lord and husband Agamemnon. Waited for justice. For revenge. The chance to kill a king.

At the base of the plaza's half circle behind Clytæmnestra, the girl erupts from the forest path, chest heaving, nostrils (both ringed and unringed) flared, blue eyes wide and white with searching. Spots Clytæmnestra. Stops short. Relieved. Pauses to catch her breath without withdrawing her gaze from the old woman.

This is Suzy Creamcheez. Difficult to tell her age because she conforms to none of the ready-made female models. Young, yes, a great deal younger than Clytæmnestra, whom she has followed here. But not a girl. Hasn't been a girl for some time now. Torn jungle-green shorts over black tights, standard worn-down black-and-white hightops, and sleeveless greyish T-shirt under a paisley waistcoat straight from the Sally Ann, bare arms and shoulders, muscular and tanned and thickened by the sting of mosquitoes and the slash of the underbrush. You'd expect the shaved head and the three rings dangling from her pierced nose to complete the tough look she's obviously going for; instead, they evoke a kind of fragility.

Slowly and with an exaggerated air of nonchalance, Suzy saunters along the crescent's edge, stretching her arms like some morning jogger casually surveying the city. She stops a good ten yards away from Clytæmnestra, beside one of the three large silver binoculars on black posts, which the Parks Department has provided for the benefit of those who, having trudged all the way up to the lookout for a long view, are willing to pay a handful of coins for the illusion of being once more down on the street whence they came. Suzy has no coin, but she crouches slightly and pretends to look through the spyglass, aiming first at the set of manmade islands in the middle of the river and then sweeping past the dilapidated remnants of pavilions from the long-gone World's Fair, over the amusement park covered in the old grease of french fries and hot dogs and the dust of sugar candy, then swinging back to the Casino, still ablaze from the night's gambling. Grabbing hold of the binoculars with both hands, Suzy sprays the scene with the simulated rat-tat-tat of a machine gun and the whistle and crash of rockets. Clytæmnestra, showing no sign of noticing, continues to stare out at the earth's curvature, murmuring softly. Suzy breaks off her antics, straightens up and, pouting slightly, drapes herself over the binoculars. She knows better than to interrupt.

Twenty-five centuries on these ramparts, watching for the enemy. Who knows the horizon better than I do? The towers of Troy piled against the black river. Black river running past, to Aulis, where he murdered my Iphigenia for a breath of wind and a war. Who better than I knows the city below? City of daily life, war in a briefcase, death in a raincoat folded over your arm.

11

Clytæmnestra's arms float slowly up to shoulder height. Her hands, stretching to either side, begin to flap gently.

What do you see, Clytæmnestra?

I see everything. Nothing escapes my gaze. My eyes on the horizon. Her eyes on me. The thin line where earth meets sky. The soft blur between world and heaven. The future where hope collides with death. Twenty-five centuries I've watched that line. Watching for ruin, waiting for an army of Amazons to avenge their Hippolyta and free us from this mountain of mud.

What do you see, Clytæmnestra?

I see nothing. The future, the armies of change, have all been swept into the sea. Only we remain. Last tattered band of heroes. Crippled, sick and dying, half-crazed from the sound of our own voices echoing off the steel glass towers below.

Very slowly, Clytæmnestra begins to spin, arms extended, hands fluttering. Suzy takes one step closer, away from the binoculars, still not interfering but alert. Large, isolated raindrops begin to lay a random pattern of dark flecks across the paving stones.

Shh, Clytæmnestra. Be quiet. Why torment yourself? Come away from there. There's nothing to see.

I see what I see. And should I not say so? Who will stop my mouth? Who will silence Clytæmnestra? Is that you, Orestes, come at last? Is it my son, come to murder his mother because she speaks? Speaks what? The truth? A dream? What does it matter, so long as she speaks?

Now the fit of asterixis is upon her: faster and faster she spins, arms floating, hands flapping wildly, eyes staring into the blur, shouting:

How long now? How many years? Searching the sky for a sign, a torch, a star? How many years now? How many more?

Spinning round and round, breathless and raging, and the rain pouring down, washing over dark shining stones, over Suzy's bare head and her shoulders, over Clytæmnestra's pale spinning face, until finally she collapses, falls into Suzy's waiting arms, weak and panting for air. Exhausted. The rain shower passes.

Season of Mud

Back in the camp, Clytæmnestra slips her arm free without so much as a smile of thanks (and yet, just before the moment of separation, wasn't that an ever-so-slight pressure Suzy felt against her breast?) and walks straight-backed and proud to her bed, a makeshift shelter patched together from scraps of wood and tin and branches. The forest is dotted with perhaps a dozen similar constructions, but following the long, pitiless winter only the sturdiest are still occupied. The remainder have been scavenged for materials.

Clytæmnestra's lean-to is not the most elaborate, but over the years it has acquired a degree of solidity, if not permanence. For roofing, most of the shelters use the best and cheapest defense against the rain: old plastic shower curtains. These have the disadvantage that they can sometimes be spotted through the trees, certainly from above, but even occasionally from the streets below—in a glance through a windshield up over the traffic jam, in the midst of a cool gaze from the window of a skyscraper surveying the universe at the observer's disposal; in a bovine stare between mouthfuls of tuna salad from the flaked green edge of a park bench. Suddenly, a glimpse of bright orange curlicues, a patch of purple ducks, yellow fish. Most city dwellers, busy with their own affairs, blink and move on. A few—on the short-term plan, scraping by, alert to after-sundown options—are more likely to read and interpret the kitschy signs. But the real danger comes from those in the pay of law and order and the Parks Department. The shower curtains are a liability. Still, the advantages, especially during this season of rain, outweigh the risks.

The other inhabitants of the camp have not begun to stir. Only Lady Macbeth is busy cooking something which, on closer examination, turns out to be only water boiling in a battered tin pot over a small fire. Suzy crouches beside the fire, warming her hands, watching.

Lady Macbeth, circling her pot, draws and tightens the ratty bathrobe round her faded nightgown, pokes and fusses nervously at the discarded food wrappers and precious dry twigs that feed her flame, mutters an incantation, passes a blackened hand across her forehead, shuts for a moment her dark insomniac eyes. Circles the fire. Her long tight braids swinging in time to her chant.

Spring, you say. The end of winter. New life. The earth reborn verdant, clean and freshly innocent. Shit. Spring is the season of mud. Mud everywhere, on our hands, our faces, clinging to the outside of our boots and the inside of our lungs. The camp mired. Above: grey-brown clouds, an occasional rain shower hammering our shelters like a migraine, more grey-brown clouds. And more rain. Filthy black rain streaking down out of a shit-brown dirty sky. And the camp, shit-brown and dirty, rising up to meet the falling heavens, obliterating any line between earth and sky, any horizon.

Could this be heaven, then, at last? Heaven and earth, one thick brown streak across the horizon. These murky figures being introduced, could they be angels in paradise? And what do angels do in paradise all through the eternity of neither-day-nor-night? What would you do?

Fight to stay dry. Try to quench your thirst. Search for clean water. Suck the beads of clear water off the surface of a leaf, from the crook of a branch. Hunt for dry twigs and dead leaves. Try to make a fire to burn the damp out of your clothes. Comb the worms and squirmy larvae that drop from the trees out of your hair. Keep your things covered and out of the rain: a notebook, a pen, a toothbrush, the last of the matches, toilet paper, that photo of you and a child whose name you don't remember. Scrape the dry, caked-on muck off your boots. Crawl into the thick of the woods and crouch down, shivering, to shit. Wash the past from your hands.

Heaven? The life of angels?

A helicopter on traffic watch makes a pass over the park.

Clytæmnestra, weakened by her morning seizure, settles into her hammock. Suzy edges near. "You going down to the city later?" she asks.

Clytæmnestra turns her dark gaze on the girl.

"Just asking," Suzy says. "I might go down."

"I work alone," says Clytæmnestra, turning away.

Lady Macbeth raises her eyes from her bubbling pot.

No, not paradise. And no angels these. Certainly not Lady Macbeth. Not Clytæmnestra.

Were we men, kings for example, then heaven's gates might have swung wide to welcome us. Were we men, what would it matter how many we had butchered? Did not Zeus himself bind his own father?

But these are women. Murdering women. Long, dark-eyed women full of black mysteries and cunning power and dreams of vengeance. Women to watch out for rather than over. There's no place in any paradise of our construction for king-killers. Fighters in a camp, suspended between the city and the sky, between their wild hopes and the drag-me-down mire of this stillborn spring. Guerrilla limbo. Caught between the cross and the city below. Crossed out, double-crossed, transported, collected, condemned to scrabble up and down this Mont-Royal, this worn-down mountain, really no more than a muddy hill, a city's shrugging shoulder.

And what of the city below? Getting on with its business, working day-to-day, up in the morning and home to bed at night. Oblivious to their revolution. How long now? How many years? Searching the sky for a sign, a torch, a star. How many years now? How many more?

Suzy crouches by the fire. Watches Lady Macbeth toss a handful of crushed linden leaves into the pot and the water turn a liquid gold. Listens to the grumbling of her sisters. Waits for tea and a chance at love.

Calling Red Bandits

The camp is quiet. Only the crackle of Lady Macbeth's fire, the harping of a stubborn thrush, the drip of winter dying in the trees. Then, from somewhere on the perimeter, a loud static burst. Someone fiddling with the antenna on a transmitter, a long wire winding through the branches overhead and up toward the Cross.

Ernesto Guevara, bent and bearded in his worn-out fatigues and beret with its pinkish star, barks into the mike: "This is Red Sierra. Red Sierra calling los rebeldes. I repeat, HQ calling red bandits. This is HQ calling. Come in, los rebeldes, come in. Over."

No response.

"Red Sierra calling red bandits. Can you hear me, Joaquin? Come in, Joaquin, come in. Over."

White noise.

Clytæmnestra, supine upon her hammock, shakes her head. "Rien à faire."

"Rien à faire," Suzy echoes.

Guevara turns toward the women. "I heard that," he growls. "We'll have none of your unproductive cynicism."

"Un…productive cynicism," chants Suzy, lapsing into one of her occasional spells of echolalia.

Guevara snorts, turns back to the radio. Every morning—for almost a half century—he has doggedly scanned the airwaves for a sign of Joaquin's band. Still no contact. Nothing since Ché split the group in two and put Joaquin in charge of the rearguard. Yet another mistake? Have the others all been wiped out? Surrendered? Is this the last zone of resistance? No way of knowing. The radio might be broken. If only he could make contact, prove the existence of just one fighter out there. As it is, no use denying it, morale is critically low. They are surrounded, their numbers dwindling.

Discipline is…nil. He's lost any control he might once have had over the group. Do they even recognize his leadership? And he—Ernesto Guevara de la Serna, doctor of leprology and revolutionary archaeologist, Jesuit priest of warfare, American El Cid, Martin Fierro of the Pampas, Don Quixote of the Gauchos, last of the barbudos, guerrillero heroico, Comandante of Ciro Redondo Column 8—*El Ché* reduced to nagging at a handful of women. There are moments when he wishes he could forget about them, let go the reins and let the beast wander where it will. But without leadership, what hope of victory? Not that he's some sort of automaton. A bottle of rum, a bowl of yerba maté, a good book of poems, Lorca, Neruda…who else here can quote Baudelaire by heart, and in the original French? *A ce soldat brisé! s'il faut qu'il désespère / D'avoir sa croix et son tombeau; / Ce pauvre agonisant que déjà le loup flaire!* Clearly, the problem is morale. What's really needed is a fundamental rectification. An ideological cleansing within the ranks. A war on petit-bourgeois defeatism. But some contact on the radio would help.

Static.

Suzy yawns. Stretches. "If he'd let me try, I bet I could get some music on that thing."

Clytæmnestra laughs, really just a single cough cut off before it clears her throat. "They don't like to share their toys."

"Aren't you supposed to be on lookout?" Ché shouts back through the electric haze. They ought, he tells himself, to understand the inevitability of the present difficulties. And then, though he knows better, shouts: "We are revolutionaries. Even in a period of reflux, our duty is to be continuously aware, alert, prepared to grasp changes in the relations of forces." His voice rises, gaining momentum, sailing through the trees and over the city. "Once begun, the revolutionary process must never cease nor pause to rest. True revolutionaries do not wait for objective conditions to produce a miracle." In full flight, his voice deep and rich, the words pouring forth, the old power. "We are not mere puppets on the strings of History. Be bold, comrades…"

Suzy joins in. "The duty of a revolutionary is to make revolution!" but she is going alone now, and by heart; Ché has suddenly broken off, as though he has lost his place in the text.

As though a door has slammed shut in his brain. He struggles to regain his train of thought. Then, breathless, almost whispering, sets off again: "She was sitting in the garden, on a white cane lounging chair, her legs long and bent together, her eyes gazing out beyond the shore. I had been in swimming. My hair was wet, my arms... I was cold, shivering..."

He stops. Recovers. Shakes his head, squints in concentration. "A revolution which ceases to renew itself is a revolution in regression. The combatants tire, begin to lose hope, fall prey to the sugar-coated bullets of the enemy..."

And then again, the switch is thrown. "Sewing... She was sewing a button, the long white sleeves of my shirt draped over her knees... I pulled my feet through the shallow water, shivering. I called to her..."

He swings an arm in front of his face, as if to clear the cobwebs, shouts: "Now, more than ever, is the time to march firmly along the path already outlined, confidently and firmly dedicated to achieving victory and consolidating the... the... consolidating the... I spoke to her, and she nodded, her hair swinging across her cheek, her lips tightly pressed together... She whispered: *Ernestito... Ernestito...* softly whispering, *Teté...*"

Ché pauses, confused, checks his watch. Reaches, in a gesture of pure habit, into the right-hand pocket of his tattered fatigues and pulls out his Ventolin inhaler, an old busted blue pump held together with yellowed tape and long since empty of medicine. Almost unconsciously, he brings the machine to his mouth and pumps two quick bursts of stale nothing into his lungs before shoving it back into his pocket.

"Comrades, what is needed is a gesture. Something to remind the people that the revolution lives. Something to upset the peaceful slumber of the reactionaries."

"We are the stuff of nightmares," Lady Macbeth murmurs.

"Yes," Clytæmnestra agrees, "but the city has long since ceased to dream."

"We must carry the war to wherever the enemy is: to his home, to his place of amusement; to make it total. He must be denied a moment's peace, not a quiet moment outside nor even within his barracks. I am proposing a raid," Ché says. "A single, swift, well-planned action."

"Into the streets with poems and guns," Clytæmnestra laughs.

"You will have time to look at the stars when the worms are eating you at their leisure," Ché barks, tossing Lorca back at her Neruda.

Lady Macbeth stands, stirring stick in hand, and strikes a pose. "Blow wind! Come wrack! At least we'll die with harness on our back."

Ché takes a step toward her. "I need volunteers."

"Volunteers," Suzy calls, dangling from her branch.

"Who has the courage to change the world?" Ché wants to know. "To risk his life for…"

"…her," Suzy interrupts, "to risk *her* life."

Ché swallows and begins again. "To risk his or her life for the future."

"Hand me the man-axe, someone, hurry!" Clytæmnestra declaims skyward from her bunk.

"If I get no volunteers, comrades, I shall have to name some." No sooner has the threat been issued than he regrets it.

"Fie, my lord, fie! A soldier, and afeard?" Lady Macbeth whispers over her pot.

"Now, once more, who will join me? Who will strike a blow? A quick raid. One police station, a post office…"

"The Dairy Queen," suggests Suzy.

Ché retreats to his bunk, to silence and to tinkering with the radio. He knows perfectly well how ridiculous he appears. Wild dreaming, crazy schemes. It's all right there in the cherry-coloured diary. "October 8. Defeat." Certainly the revolution has failed. His call to arms drowned out by peals of laughter. Where are the masses? Glued to their television sets, weeding green lawns, barbecuing in the garden. History dissolved in a blue-chip cocktail.

And yet, no. Outside the tightening ring of privilege, beyond the safety of the pink-skinned suburbs, dark ragged mobs of hunger gather. She stood up, swinging around to take the blue towel from the back of her chair. In the favelas, the barrios, drinking foul water and picking in the city's mountain of garbage, skeletal caravans trekking across African deserts, Western war surplus, bones and empty eyes. She walked barefoot across the soft grass to meet me, displaying the towel before her like a matador's work cape. Their numbers are growing. Soon they will be at the city's gates. Meanwhile, within the very core of a few safe havens, the hungry, the destitute, without work or dignity, with neither heat nor clean water, jammed together in the wretched hovels of the inner city, begging for scraps with their backs against the shop windows and their eyes on the passing indifference of the rich. Wrapped me in the towel, rubbing my back, my arms, my chest. And the children: angry, hardened, dope-pushing, gun-toting gangs. A school of tiny minnows swept past, then abruptly changed direction in perfect unison, like an outstretched hand fanning the water before her. Today, they are mad scorpions tearing at each other, preying on the poor, but tomorrow, tomorrow, they will come pouring out of the ghettos, bursting through your television screens and tramping blood, your blood, over your deep-piled carpets and pristine sheets, stepping into the shallow water, lifting her skirt, her long long legs... Is no one willing to follow me down?...down...down to the water to wait for me, her pale ankles beneath the water's surface, her toes buried beneath the sand.

Has he been thinking to himself or shouting again at the top of his lungs? No way to tell. Clytæmnestra still on her back, Lady Macbeth poking at her fire. Indifferent. Not even an argument.

"Someone's coming," Suzy announces from the top of a chin-up.

Immediately Ché is on his feet and scrambling toward her. "How many? Are they armed? On foot?" He spins around, calling to the others, "Condition Yellow!" and then back to Suzy, who has dipped down again the length of her arms. "How far away?"

Suzy remains unperturbed. "Just one so far. Can't tell the sex. Running up the bridle path." Her arms bend.

Ché turns and shouts at Clytæmnestra, who has not budged from her bed, "Condition Yellow! Battle stations!" then back to Suzy, "Alone, you say? Could it be one of ours?"

Suzy pauses a moment with her chin above the bar. "It's a woman. Wearing some kind of uniform...a track suit."

"A messenger," says Ché, moving to the edge of the bushes. "With news from Joaquin." He can see movement through the trees. He raises a hand and, just to be sure, declares "Condition Red!"

Clytæmnestra yawns audibly. Lady Macbeth tastes her broth. Suzy drops to the ground. "It's just a jogger," she says, brushing past Ché and across to Clytæmnestra's side.

He freezes, his back to the camp, his hand still raised in red alert. The adrenaline mix of fear and hope rushing through his swollen veins. The familiar bile-green wave swelling up before him. Scrapes together a deep breath and waits to emerge on the other side. "A jogger," he says, his voice thin and hoarse. "We've warned them about that. We ought to shoot one. Then maybe they'd close off the damn road." Walks back to his post. Mutters to no one in particular, "Cancel Condition Red," and squats down by his bunk, too tired to do anything but flip the switch on the radio.

The traffic helicopter makes another pass through the light drizzle.

White noise.

Pointe-à-Callière

Morning down by the river. A single rusting freighter bobs idly by the loading docks. A few gulls wheel over the old port, defecate on the empty grain elevators and spin away laughing toward the city centre. In the wake of the birds, silence; only the rush of water and the drone of muttered prayers. The praying comes from a trench at the foot of an abandoned tower, not far from the spot known as Pointe-à-Callière. Here, in a dark slash of still frozen ground—the remains of an abandoned archaeological dig, more or less covered in clear plastic and pale slats of wood—Paul de Chomedey, sieur de Maisonneuve, devoted emissary of the Société de Notre-Dame de Montréal pour la conversion des sauvages de la Nouvelle-France, founder of the Mission at Hochelaga and (until Jesuit scheming got the better of him) Governor of Montréal, has taken refuge through the winter. He rarely leaves his monk's cell, bare but for an old bible, a crucifix and a pallet lined with yellowed newspapers and wet dreams of the Virgin. Though old and weary, he still wears the frayed cuffs, ragged sleeves and muddied trousers of what was once the clean unmarked and undecorated uniform of a seventeenth-century soldier. Three hundred and fifty desperate winters, the iron-tight Iroquois shackles round his camp and the bacilli of treason multiplying within the barricades have all combined to grind uniform, hair and lungs down to the same cineral grey. Still, monsieur le Gouverneur clings to his mission with all the breathless ferocity of a tubercular cough. "Faith," he reminds the monstrous city behind him. "Faith is our only weapon."

"Nonsense. Faith has nothing to do with it." De Maisonneuve is not alone. The other man who shares the trench is a Swiss, Le Corbusier, né Charles-Édouard Jeanneret, leading figure of the international modern movement in architecture, creator of the Maison Dom-Ino, the Radiant City and Chandigarh. His appearance is fastidious, although the slicked-back hair, round wire-rimmed glasses, bow-tie and black evening jacket have all seen better days.

The two men have little in common, except perhaps this fear of flooding which keeps them busy fortifying their encampment against the river. Le Corbusier has allowed his difficult circumstances to dampen neither his discipline nor his confidence in the future. He has made the best of his section of the trench, smoothing out the earthen walls and fabricating a kind of drafting table out of what was once a refrigerator door. It's not Ronchamp, but his spirit remains unbroken. He has been up and working since the early dawn, absorbed in a mass of architectural plans and diagrams. "Science requires not faith but rather a clear head and a logical approach."

De Maisonneuve's attempt to respond disintegrates into a bone-breaking coughing fit. The dog Pilote, third occupant of the encampment, shifts his tired bones and curls back to sleep in the corner. The coughing goes on for several minutes before Le Corbusier's concentration is finally disturbed, at which point, without a glance at his trenchmate, he abandons his drawing board to slip on his once white, now grey, gloves, gather up his plastic bags, load up his converted three-wheeled bicycle and cart and set out for a late breakfast. The grey cobbled streets of Old Montreal are still empty, but the public garbage receptacles, baskets fashioned in wrought iron and wood and strategically located on every second corner, are stuffed with last night's feasting.

Le Corbusier collects things. But not just any thing; he searches out the geometrical forms of standardized objects: beer cans, wine or pop bottles, pens, pencils, plastic disposables of all kinds. He trades these for money, of course, but the pleasure comes in gathering them up and then, following that initial examination to confirm their flawless condition, patiently rubbing them clean and aligning them carefully in the plastic bag with which he has lined the basket on his vehicle. Each item is treasured, lovingly reclaimed from the detritus of the city. Le Corbusier remains secure in the knowledge that the only true and moral pleasure can be found in the basic necessities: a loaf of bread, a salami. The fountain pen, the briar pipe, the bowler hat, the wine bottle, the flask, the column, the ever-sharp pencil, the typewriter, the telephone, the filing cabinet, the plate-glass window, the limousine, the laboratory, the hospital, the gymnasium, the safety razor. Culture, after all, is an orthogonal state of mind. Man is a geometrical animal! Triangles, rectangles, the perfect circle, the pyramid, the prism: these are the pure, clean shapes of progress, the products of natural selection. Whereas nature is an imperfect artist, disorderly, realizing greatness only in happy moments when she accidentally produces perfect bodies, such as the crystal. A rectilinear geometry is functional for speed, and beautiful because clear. An elementary geometry disciplines the masses: the square, the cube, the sphere. Visual deceits, eclectic styles are to be found in socially degenerate situations such as the Turkish bazaar, filthy and noisy, based on theft, lying, and systematic, stylistic fakery. Decoration is disease and crime.

Stop. Le Corbusier has been thinking out loud. Possibly shouting. Again. Thankfully, he is alone in the street. Place Jacques-Cartier, outside the Hotel Nelson. His back to the river. The cobbled rectangular plaza sloping up between the old stone houses remade into restaurants and native crafts shops, up to the staircase of the Hôtel de Ville staring down at him like some palatial church from the top of the hill. A cold wind lashes at his ankles and wrists. He works fast, trying, as he digs, to ignore the half-eaten semisolids, the slime-drenched papers, scum-crumpled napkins. The viscera. There. A beer can. But no, this one is irreparably damaged, crushed into a jagged irregular aberration. He moves on. Here the trash baskets are more numerous, one every fifty yards. Le Corbusier continues his digging, gathering cans, plastic forks and spoons, unbroken straws. And then, halfway up the plaza, in the gutter amid the overflow of a basket, a small black film canister. He examines it closely. A clean undamaged cylinder. Exactly what he has been looking for. The perfect container for Modulor. At the north end of the plaza, a figure appears, slowly working from bin to bin. Quickly Le Corbusier pockets the canister, and hurries on to the next can, pushing his cart before him.

At first, from a distance, Le Corbusier is almost certain he recognizes his trenchmate de Maisonneuve. Finally come out of his hole? But, no, that would be impossible. De Maisonneuve would not come out of his fortifications to collect empties; monsieur le Gouverneur does not engage in trade. His spirit is invested elsewhere. Mainly he is on the lookout for a sign, a sign that God has not abandoned his mission at Montréal. A sign plus anything to reinforce his encampment against the encroaching waters.

And then, as the number of baskets between them diminishes, Le Corbusier realizes this scavenger is not de Maisonneuve at all. How could he have imagined any similarity? Except for the dark clothing and the obvious indigence, this one has nothing in common with his friend. The shaved head, the rings and tattoos—some sort of punker horning in on his territory. He's seen them on rue Sainte-Catherine, small pockets of leather and spiked hair, has heard about their music, wild dancing, graffiti, violence. Le Corbusier hesitates, takes a step backward, checks round the empty square for witnesses, police, an open doorway—teenagers without respect or morals or ethics or the slightest sense of history, this one too, that way of swaggering, the arms slightly akimbo…my God…it's a woman.

His rising panic evaporates and is replaced by a kind of outrage. Who does she think she is? He begins striding toward her, leaving his tricycle behind. This, his territory, his bins, every morning now for in excess of four decades, no one ever…he stops short, squints up at the top of the block, along la rue Notre-Dame past the Hôtel de Ville. No one. He tries to recall; do they travel in gangs? But this one seems to be alone. An advance scout? Thin edge of the wedge. Better not take any chances. Put a stop to it. Nip it in the bud. Rapidly, he adjusts his bow-tie, smoothes his jacket and closes the distance between them.

Either she hasn't spotted him or has decided to ignore him, concentrating instead on the contents of this, the third trash can from the north end of the plaza.

"Look here," he says, almost adding "young lady" but catching himself in time, "what's the meaning of this?"

Suzy glances up. "Meaning," she repeats, nodding. "What's the meaning," and continues her rummaging.

Her technique, he notes, is deplorable: unstructured and untidy. "What do you think you're looking for?"

Suzy shrugs. "Not meaning." She pulls an empty beer can from the basket and jams it into her backpack.

"Stop that!" With a sudden, almost involuntary gesture, Le Corbusier reaches out and grabs her arm. Instantly Suzy pulls out of his grasp and takes a fighting stance. "This is…my place," he says.

"This is my place," Suzy echoes, injecting just a touch more of the whining tone that he immediately realizes was already present.

He tries for something more authoritative: "Look at the mess you've made," but even before she repeats it, he knows it sounds like nagging.

Suzy turns to survey the garbage strewn across the paving stones and, thanks to the wind, already drifting into ever-widening circles around the three bins she has left in her wake. She shrugs. "Neatness doesn't count."

"You'll have the police down on me." It's not so much her stealing his goods that he minds, although that's part of it, but the disruption of his routine. And the nonchalance. "I have," he continues, "over the years, established good relations with the local authorities…"

"Years of authority…" echoes Suzy.

"You, coming here without regard for anyone's prior claims, with your disrespectful attitude, your slovenly habits, outrageous appearance…"

"Outrageous appearance…"

"Well, I'm very sorry, but it won't do, won't do at all. You shall simply have to go elsewhere…what are you doing? Come here. Stay away from that."

Suzy, bored with his diatribe, has moved around the architect, and is walking toward his vehicle. Le Corbusier hurries after her.

"Neat," she says, kneeling to admire the gear system on the tricycle.

Le Corbusier puts a proprietary hold on the handlebars. "Don't touch that; it's very delicate."

"Don't worry, I won't break your toy." She gives the machinery a last appreciative glance and stands back.

Le Corbusier breathes easier; perhaps his dark premonitions about this creature were premature: the danger, if there was any, seems to have passed. He clears his throat. "Allow me to present myself. Perhaps you have heard of Le Corbusier." (This last not a question.) "La Maison Citrohan, the Nestlé Pavilion, the Mundaneum, l'Unité d'habitation in Marseille, Ronchamp, Chandigarh." Nothing. No reaction. He persists. Something compels him to fill her reactive void with his accomplishments. "The Dom-Ino, ribbon windows, curved walls, interior ramps, brises-soleil, pivoting doors, undulating roofs, the free plan, le béton brut."

"Béton brut." Suzy stares past him to the grain elevators and the river beyond.

Le Corbusier pauses for breath, follows her gaze. "Yes, these glorious concrete towers are our cathedrals. Our pyramids."

"I'm not crazy about this city," Suzy murmurs almost to herself.

"The city is the crack of a whip. Death for dreamers. A place of champions and gladiators, an assembly of cannibals who establish the dogma of the moment. The streets are paved with corpses. The city is a selectioner. The city designed Le Corbusier."

"Cannibals and corpses," Suzy says, tilting toward the downtown core.

"Yes, of course," Le Corbusier continues, "today the city is in decay. Black with soot and rotting from within: our neighbourhoods, our streets, our institutions, nos vies, nos cœurs, nos pensées. That, my child, is the result of centuries of stagnation and moral degradation."

"Nos cœurs stagnants. Nos cœurs stagnants." Her echolalia always seems to get worse as the emotional temperature of her surroundings rises.

"I warned them: we live in the machine age. Science and technology have placed gigantic resources at our disposal."

"Disposal," shouts Suzy, raising her own voice to match his.

"We need men of intrepid spirit, animated by civic enthusiasm and a sincere love of humanity. This is the age of the Architect-Philosopher. The fusion of art and science is become possible thanks to industrial methods of design and production."

"Civic art. Love of production."

"Now is the time to transform our cities, to conceive a new city, the city of today: magnificent, stately, efficient, practical. A city for heroes. A city of harmony through gigantic works, standardization, mass production. The Radiant City." His voice is rising, his hands make sharp slicing motions in the air.

Suzy takes a step back, alert to any possible trouble. Still she continues to respond like a distorted audio mirror: "Radiant heroes."

Le Corbusier addresses the skyscrapers behind her. "I offered to build it for them. The Radiant City. There, in the Capital of the Enlightenment, astride the Seine. A cruciform. Walls of light, pure geometric forms and pristine white surfaces."

"Walls of light. Pristine cruciform."

"In the centre of the great cross, the captains of industry, sixty-storey glass and steel towers of omniscient power. A vast city in a continuous park."

"A city," Suzy shouts back, "in a parking lot."

Le Corbusier ignores her. His own logorrhea has kicked in. "I could have done it. All I asked was the complete demolition of the Right Bank. The whole thing. A clean sweep." His voice dips to a whisper. "They refused. And why? Because they understand nothing of creation. Nothing. They fear progress, tremble in the face of destiny; show them the future and they flood their trousers." And shouting again: "They are all mired in servility, imitation, laziness, senility."

"Lazy senility!" screams Suzy.

Le Corbusier takes a step backward. "You accuse me of being fanatical. I tell you, soon they will come begging on their knees. When the inhabitants of their great towns are dying of suffocation, falling like leaves, drowning in their own refuse, they will come to Le Corbusier for salvation."

"Standardize! Rationalize!" shouts Suzy, improvising, "Ferro-concrete will be our paradise!"

This outburst seems to silence Le Corbusier. Or perhaps he has simply run out of steam. For a moment the two stand quietly, face to face, by the trash bin. Then Suzy says, "I should get going," and turns back toward the north side of Place Jacques-Cartier.

She moves west along Notre-Dame, loping easily to the rattle of tin cans in her backpack, turning south again on Saint-Sulpice toward rue de la Commune and Place Royale. Probably she ought to head downtown and beg some coins on la Catherine, but she knows if she were to head that way, she would not be able to keep from searching out Clytæmnestra. Besides, she can feel the presence of the river, the water pulling her south.

Le Corbusier waits until she is out of sight and then, pulling the small film canister from his pocket, examines it once more, carefully, before putting it safely away. He wipes his spectacles, which have fogged over after the emotional outpouring, bends quickly to rub two damp fingers over a spot of dirt on the toe of his left shoe, and returns to his excavations.

Subterranean Homesick and Blue

Le métro Berri-de-Montigny, like some great steel cruciform, the shadow of that other cross, the one atop Mount Royal, lies buried in the city's centre, as though a stake had been thrust straight through the hard paved surface of the streets and deep into Montreal's soft clay heart. Berri-de-Montigny, the intersection of the two main subway lines. Above and astride the station, wings unfurled and talons piercing down to seize the subway in their grasp, are the city's bus depot—lunch counter, plastic benches, the infamous washrooms—and l'UQAM, that most urban of universities, product of Quebec's not-so-Quiet Revolution. The trains pull in and out, the station floods and empties, a set of lungs, drawing in shoppers, white-collar workers, students, and pumping them out. Everyone is in a hurry; Berri is no one's destination, just a place of transit. In short, a fine spot for a pickpocket to earn her daily bread. The rewards may be richer in the stations to the west, but the traffic and confusion here make the work less dangerous.

On the staircase leading down from Sainte-Catherine, Clytæmnestra bends carefully to gather up another abandoned transfer. She works her way systematically through all the trash containers in the corridor, but they offer only odd newspaper sections and crumpled tissue. The corridors leading to the bus terminal and the university are lined with knickknack stores, five-and-ten-cent joints, snack bars, pinball parlours, but she prefers to work the métro. She tries three tattered transfers before one gets her through the turnstile and she can make her way down to the westbound platform of the Angrignon Park line, checking all the bins as she goes. A couple of tin cans and a bottle. Clytæmnestra does not bother with them.

She reaches the platform moments after the train has pulled out and the gallery is empty. Here, with all the jostling and hurry, the odds are usually in her favour. Three trash containers: in the third she finds a cigarette pack containing a handful of cigarettes and a Bic lighter. A mistake committed in the rush to make the train? A sudden eco-resolution? No matter. She does not smoke. She pockets the lighter and considers, for a moment, tossing the cigarettes back, but decides to keep them for Suzy. She sits with a sigh of relief on the bench along the wall and studies the people as they begin to gather on the platform. Several teenagers—no, their jeans pockets are too tight and they never stand still; a small, tweedy grey-haired woman with tight red lips in a face full of powder, carrying an Ogilvy department store bag—tempting but too careful, a tight clutcher; and then, there, just coming off the escalator: a large soft-fleshed male with wild grey hair and unruly beard, loose-fitting jacket, crumpled tie, thick glasses, one strap of his leather bag hanging free, badly worn shoes, and that bovine expression suggesting he is elsewhere, a professor solving differential equations or concocting his next government grant proposal—perfect.

The briefcase will be crammed full of tiny scripted, rigorously useless notes, one or two unreadable books in first and final editions, chewed and broken pencils, rusting paper clips. Debris. She ignores it. Instead, as he moves down the platform toward her, she concentrates on the jacket pockets, loosely flapping in the tunnel's stale breath. Perhaps more Kleenex, a leaky pen, a wallet. Ah, yes, the left pocket. She works up a good quantity of saliva in her mouth and spits it onto the fingers of her right hand. Then she bends over and drags her hand along the ground in the space between the bench and the wall where the oldest and greatest amount of dirt has accumulated. She sloshes another mouthful of spittle over the result to make the sludge in her hand more lively, and leaves her seat. A roar sounds distantly from the tunnel at the end of the platform.

"Spare change?" Clytæmnestra mutters, startling the prof out of his funding daydreams. He hesitates, starts to move around her, glances toward the mouth of the tunnel. The blunt nose of the train appears, filling the dark hole at the north end of the station. Head down, she shifts slightly to block his way. Finally, rapidly, he fumbles in his trouser pocket and produces some loose coins—a quarter, two nickels, a penny— offers them. Already the blue cars are flashing alongside—pale blue smudge broken by pale faces, dark coats, a bare arm held high. Now, with a sudden, rapid gesture, Clytæmnestra extends her filthy palm up and close to his face. He looks, takes a quick step back, and turning slightly, focuses all his attention on laying the money in her hand without actually touching the bubbling scum. The slimy palm the train huffing and wheezing slowing to a stop meanwhile her other hand clean and quick fishing the wallet from the pocket of his jacket. The doors part. They are engulfed in the crowd pouring out of the train. He slides past her into the car, turns to face her through the open door, patting his pockets in a gesture typical of the absent-minded. Stops. Freezes, one hand on his jacket pocket, the elbow bent (so that the powder-faced lady in tweed is momentarily put off balance and driven back tightlipped into her déclassé ruminations). Three warning notes sound from the head of the train. The professor jams his hand into the pocket, fingers stretching into the lint-infested corners. The doors kiss, his head jerks up and, through the glass, for a single instant, his eyes, wide with terrible understanding, lock onto the dark ancient orbs of the once great Queen of Argos. Then he's gone. A blur. Clytæmnestra gathers up her dress and proceeds straight-backed and regal along the platform toward the exit.

In a twisted nook in the tunnel leading to rue Sainte-Catherine, she takes stock. A few illegible scraps of paper containing what might be phone numbers or dates, a driver's license — expired — a ragged inter-library card, an ID with a photograph of a younger, cleaner version of her victim, a bank card, and a credit card which, a few decades ago, she might have parlayed into something in one of the big department stores, but now, thanks to her appearance, is useless. And that's it. Absolutely no cash. The idiot forgot to stop by the bank machine. She pockets the library card (the promise of a warm place to sit and rest her feet some time during the next long winter) and tosses the rest in a trash bin on the way up to the washroom in the bus depot to wash her hands.

Mouth Music

Prince Arthur Street, the stretch running east of the boulevard Saint-Laurent. You have neither watch nor sun to mark the hour; only a faint sheen over the slate-grey city suggests some time a little past noon. The street appears empty, all the more so because really it is a false street. A façade. Once Prince Arthur was a treeless offshoot of The Main, a kind of hybrid of east-end Montréal and old Europe: the glass-bricked tavern straddling the north corner and spewing the sweet stench of draft into the street and up toward the windows of the Polish Sports Club on the floor above, the line of Azorean blue doors on narrow broken-down flats, the laundromat on the corner of de Bullion Street where L. C. used to spin-dry his poems, the mustachioed waiter in the window of the Mazurka Restaurant, the head-banging doorway into the secondhand bookstore crammed with suffocating dry mold and random stacks tottering between the crooked wooden floor and the low water-stained ceiling, the dépanneur next door stocking cigarettes, twenty-fours of Dow, Molson and Labatt, dented cans of Campbell's soup, past-due milk, Spam, sardines, last night's sex murders, *Echo Vedette*.

Only the Mazurka and the dépanneur have survived. The street has been closed to traffic and remade into a clean odourless Disney-Paris, a place where American tourists and suburbanites in matching pastel-coloured windbreakers and slacks can come for a taste of le Montréal français. The gaslight street lamps are really brand-new simulacra, the street itself is smoothly cobbled in machine-cut stones of pinkish hue and lined with Vietnamese and Greek restaurants spilling plastic chairs and tables garnished with Coca-Cola parasols. A few boutiques sell Expos T-shirts, chocolate-dipped soft ice cream and tin souvenirs. Here and there, a street musician, a juggler, a portrait caricaturist lounge, smoking, waiting for a chance at the odd lunch-time customer. It's too early in the season for tourists and the suburbanites only show up on weekends. Prince Arthur is an empty shell.

Almost at the end of the strip, within sight of the grass and trees and the water fountain of le carré Saint-Louis, Lady Macbeth has taken up her usual spot. A ragged square cloth of the same indeterminate colour as her bathrobe lies folded on the cobbled street to receive donations. Lady Macbeth herself paces back and forth over the few metres surrounding the cloth, now muttering to herself, now playing a small mouth organ which she carries in the pocket of her bathrobe. There is no tune, no melody, no music to her playing, only a continuous sucking and blowing on a single, unvarying block of notes. Clutching the harmonica between her lips and two fingers, she plays whether the street is full or empty. Plays for no one, least of all herself. When the occasional passerby drops a coin at her feet, she offers not even an acknowledgment in return. The Samaritan pausing for the closure of a quick smile or nod moves on with nothing to show for his efforts and his cash. Lady Macbeth marches to her bisyllabic rhythm. Back and forth. Sucking in. Blowing out. A kind of primary breathing exercise. Marking time, the progress of her existence. In past summers, once she had collected two dollars and thirty-five cents from the tourists, she would go into the old Mazurka for a goulash soup and a buttered slice of brown bread. But now, in the empty street, she paces. Over the same ground again and again. Sucking in, blowing out. Or, removing the instrument from her mouth and slipping it into the pocket of her robe, her emptied hands turn in and out of each other in a relentless Möbius movement. Recitation.

The sleeping silence in the castle. And the cold. The cold of stones. Waiting in the darkened chamber. The open casement. Black square of night. Moonless. I had a light. A single candle. Waiting. Nothing to do now but wait. And he gone such a long time. Why so long? How much time to cut an old man's throat? And so cold. Bone-chilling cold. Should I go up and see? Will he do it? Or falter at the last moment? Must I do this too in your stead, then? Having prepared the meal, seated the guests and laid out the cutlery, now must I also cut your meat for you? And you a soldier? How peacefully he slept. Had he not resembled my father... Shall I lift up my skirts, now, and climb the stairs?

To raise your hand in mine and guide the dagger to its mark. Or shall I wield the blade myself? To stand over a dreaming king. Frail mortal. Pale body. Powerless in sleep. And such a bird's neck, nothing but pale wrinkled skin and dry gristle, I could snap it like kindling in my hands. So little life and yet so stubborn. Who would have thought the old man had so much blood in him? It is not yet done. I might still reach him. Now it is here. The last possible moment, the edge, the brink of fate. Pulling the great stone blocks of our desire behind us, we approach the summit. In an instant we'll begin the long descent. If I went up this second. Went up and stopped your hand. Now, before the long cord of time unravels. The last instant. Stop it, now! And then what? More of the same. Waiting and spending my life a penny at a time in this grey murky purgatory. No, rather risk it all in a single throw. Strike! Be bloody, bold, and resolute; laugh to scorn the power of man. What keeps him there? For a moment, I swear it was my father lay there. What's that cry? A night owl. The moment's past. We've passed over the hump of time. Time unwinds. Fate can never be undone: to bed, to bed, to bed.

A bank teller, hurrying on her high heels and lunch break from boulevard Saint-Laurent into le carré Saint-Louis, stops and stoops over the folded cloth, nods, smiles at the braided player's prose. "Ahh, Shakespeare," she says, eyebrows arching. Drops two quarters, pauses for some response. Nothing. Lady Macbeth fumbles for her pocket. Raises the mouth organ to her lips. Sucks it in. Blows it out. Marches to her mouth music.

And Drink from the River Lethe

here are moments when she finds herself on the cobblestones between darkly brooding doorways with a bit of wind in her face, the river winking in the distance and no idea of who she's supposed to be or how she got here. Her first reaction is panic. Touching herself, mouth, bare shoulder, breast. The rings in her nose. Scanning the sidewalk for a sign. Anything. The smell of spring, wet earth and rotting turds.

A faint voice from the cracked window above her head, a phrase: "Son oncle l'a invitée dans sa maison neuve." Maison neuve. New house. A scrap of memory drifts to the surface. A kitchen: fridge, stove, cracked porcelain sink, worn tiles, the smell of fresh paint on the walls mixing in with tomato sauce and onions and, in the corner, a yellow dog standing over his yellow bowl. Pilote? For a moment she thinks that's who she might be, the yellow dog. But no. Those big eyes, the big pink tongue are wagging up at her. Pilote, whacking his tail against the cupboard door. Her dog? Her mother's kitchen? Maybe, but who is she? A small girl coming in from playing in the yard, looking to sneak a cookie before supper, before her father comes home, his tufted knuckles, the sweet stink of beer on his breath. Her name is…Jeanne, Jeanne Mance. She's seven years old. Her friend Rudy is outside waiting, if she brings the cookie he'll show her his thing and she'll be chief, they'll attack the fort, Pilote barking and jumping all over the place and knocking her down. But no, there was no dog, and no yard, Maisonneuve is the statue in the centre of Place d'Armes and Jeanne Mance is the figure beneath and to his left. And there below, a small dog pointing. Not hers. She never had a dog.

On her back, a packsack. Inside, a couple of beer cans. Returnables. That's where the sweet stink of stale beer is coming from. So she's been scavenging. Probably there is no house, no place to go. Still, she must have a name…and where is she going? A gust of wind plays in her ears. She's a dancer. She can feel the muscles in her calves, her feet arching in her boots. Yes, that's it, a dancer. Spinning tight circles on a hardwood floor. Pink leotards and tights, the smell of damp talcum powder and toe shoes, her hand gripping the bar against a wall of mirrors. She raises an arm, carves a tentative arc in the air above her head. The music building slowly, pouring down into her legs. A dancer. Yes. Maybe. A quick step and turn. She trips on her heel and crashes to the street, scraping her elbow.

So not a dancer. No, these leg muscles are not from pirouettes. A runner's legs. Running through the streets, running from what? From the law. Outlaw's legs. A courier carrying secrets back through enemy territory — keep moving, stay alert, don't stop to rest, everything depends on her getting through. The war has been going on for years. Her side is right. The people's side, the side of the oppressed, the poor, the excluded, indigent, indigenous, indignant. She is a spy, an infiltrator, that's why she's forgotten her name, she has a hundred names, like the candy wrapper there in the gutter. Her code name is O'Henry. And her information is crucial. She must get through. Down to the river where a boat, a small secret craft, is waiting to take her to the other shore. She must get to the water's edge. Everything depends on it. But what is the information she's carrying? She's forgotten that, too. Is it written somewhere, hidden on her body, in her head, in the tattoo over her heart?

The tattoo. If she could remember where she got that moon crescent etched over her left breast, then maybe the rest would fall into place. A dingy storefront plastered with navy-blue designs, a couple of hookers working the street outside, the stench of rubbing alcohol, and Rudy holding her hand. It was a gift from Rudy, her birthday. A crescent moon. For her sisters. Her name is Claire, au clair de la lune. But no, that doesn't ring a bell. If only the rain would let up, stop pouring into the river, washing away all trace of memory.

Across the street, a façade of great stone pillars: la Banque Royale. The Royal Bank. She's a queen. This is her city. She rules over a great city, stone parapets, crimson carpets, golden throne, long robes and long dark hair. She is strong and beautiful and merciless. The war is far away; she waits, ruling over a city of old men and children. Her name is Clytæmnestra. That has to be it because every time she whispers Clytæmnestra her heart skips a beat. She is Clytæmnestra and this is her city of women. But how did she get here: running through the streets in rags? Where are her robes? Her long dark hair? Her smooth dark forehead, the stretched curve of her neck, cool tight calves… No, she's not the queen; the queen is the one she loves. She's a secret lover, running from the law, in love with Clytæmnestra.

She turns down a sidestreet, back toward the river again. A siren sounds to the north. The rain washes over her face. No, definitely not a queen; an outcast, an exile. A boy cast out by his mother, on the run, making his way back home, sleeping in ditches, begging scraps on kitchen stoops, hard callused hands, sunburned arms, rings in his nose. Yes, that's it. A prince, his father's son, a boy making his way back to the city of his childhood, in rags, looking for revenge. To find his mother. Looking for his mother with a knife in his boot… Ready to battle all obstacles, that old man in black rags for example, rising out of a ditch, brandishing a busted umbrella and blocking his way to the river. Old man rising out of the ground like some ghost. His father's ghost? Swinging and swaying over the ditch… The prince pauses. Should he backtrack, take another way round? Or just kick that old man's head in?

Notre-Dame de Montréal

Paul de Chomedey prefers to remain close to home, within their walled encampment. From here he can both survey the surrounding streets and watch the river swell from the spring runoff. He keeps busy fortifying the trench with anything he can lay his hands on—rocks and sand from the trench, discarded plastic bags and bits of rubbish blown in off the street, his old journals. And praying. There being no shortage of enemies—the rising water, the Iroquois, Monseigneur Laval and his Jesuit conspirators installed downriver in the rival mission of Québec—Governor de Maisonneuve has much to pray for.

He prays to the Virgin Mary. Virgin Mary, Mother of God, Our Lady of Montréal. This is Her mission. Named, founded, dedicated in Her honour. Mission of sacrifice, seeking neither gold nor furs nor land nor power. To convert the savages to the Word of God. He asks nothing for himself, utters no complaint. He clasps his shredded, bloody knuckles and prays. Prays for the success of the mission, although, for now, all hope of converting the heathen is lost; in fact, the mission has long been reduced to defending itself against the attacks of those same savages. Still, he prays for Her glory. For the strength to serve, to remain pious, humble, celibate (in spite of the temptation of Jeanne Mance). He prays for three more centuries of selfless devotion to Her cause.

Three centuries ago, across a wild and wicked sea. Two months of summer drifting on the open water. Storms striking again and again, driving him from his appointed path. Then, at last, land. The sweet music drifting out from the mouth of the river. Stadacona. Poor greedy Stadaconians, pleading with him not to go on, to throw in with them and swell the ranks of their settlement instead, to abandon this mad Hochelaga mission with its floods, starvation, wild Iroquois.

A sudden and violent fit of coughing takes hold of de Maisonneuve, shaking and knocking him into thirty seconds of nothingness. Pilote raises his jowled head and casts a reproachful look at his master. The dog maintains his brooding stare until the fit dies down. At last, teary-eyed and exhausted, de Maisonneuve pulls himself up on his feet, wipes the trickle of blood from his mouth with a grey rag and addresses himself to the hound: "Messieurs," he says with barely enough voice to stir more than a few inches of air, "ce que vous dites serait bon si l'on m'avait envoyé pour délibérer et choisir un poste; mais la Compagnie qui m'envoie ayant déterminé que j'irais à Montréal, il est de mon honneur, et tous trouveraient bon que j'y monte pour commencer une colonie, quand tous les arbres de cette île se devraient changer en autant d'Iroquois."

Then he says no more. It's not merely that speech is physically taxing; the sound of his own voice is unbearable to him. Vain chatter. Self-absorbed yammering. Oh, how he longs for the peace of his own silence. To be free at last from ambition, pride. Desire. To abandon himself completely and irrevocably to Her; to those loving arms, that gentle bosom, golden hands, alabaster cheek, dark downcast eyes, perfect lips, to the blessed fruit of her womb.

But enough. He must not slacken. There's work to be done, shoring up the camp against the rising river. All he has left are old newspapers and rags. For the last few days, he has been eyeing Le Corbusier's drafting table, which would make a perfect wall against the water, but he is all too familiar with the architect's temper to do more than look and think. Still, such a sin, in their situation, to squander critical building materials on a luxury. He himself has only a narrow pallet for furniture. Effortless sacrifice. Riches, gold, furs, servants, the promise of a wife and family. All that was easy. And then these bare hands, this long white hair, this dark uniform stripped of all rank or decoration. The loneliness. All too easy. The sin of pride. All that attention to the self. If only… to be released from himself.

And the river is rising. For a week now, he has been charting its progress up the bank. Meanwhile he can feel the damp soaking through into the trench, the mud floor's gradual transubstantiation into water.

His work is interrupted by Pilote's warning: Iroquois. Pilote's nose is foolproof. The hound's ability to home in on the scent of Mohawk has already saved the mission in the past. Once, he would have leapt to his feet, pointing and howling. Now he offers only a sharp snort and a whimper without stirring from his slumber. But this is sufficient to alert the Governor. De Maisonneuve reaches under his bed for the stripped-down umbrella carcass, his only weapon, and scrambles to the barricade. His eyesight being what it is, the enemy is almost on them before he spots him. A lone Iroquois crossing the perimeter. A scout perhaps, small and quick and bare-scalped. No feathers or weapons visible. Coming in as though he had no idea the camp was there. As though the war had not been going on for three hundred and fifty years.

Savages drifting in from the green forest wall to greet us, their eyes full of candour and questions. We distributed among them small trinkets and bits of glass, and engaged them as guides. They led us to a clearing beneath the cliff, the place they called Tutonaguy. Through the fall, we put up homes, gardens, a wall.

But he has long since run out of trinkets…and the Mohawks out of curiosity.

Cruel Iroquois. Tides of flaming savages coming in red waves, faces smeared in their own black excrement, sex organs swollen with blood lust, godless cries in the dark night while we sleep in our beds. Night and day, from within the walled encampment, I see the painted faces, naked bodies hurling themselves at the fort.

De Maisonneuve can feel a coughing fit coming on; he struggles desperately to suppress it and pulls frantically on the bell dangling by the mouth of his trench to signal his men in from the fields. The Mohawk warrior stops coming forward, hesitates, spots him, freezes. De Maisonneuve can see him clearly now: young, no paint, but three rings dangling from the nose. The old Governor steps up and out into the open, ready to challenge, to defend the camp, to die. He waves his bones-of-an-umbrella in a slow circle above his head. The savage tenses. Edges forward. And then, suddenly, the coughing takes over: there's no more holding it back, it bursts through the dam he has willed in his throat, sweeping everything in its path.

When he recovers, he is lying on the ground outside his post, a busted umbrella and a thin line of blood by his head. The heathen is gone.

Somewhere nearby someone is drilling teeth in the street. He drags himself down into the trench to lie down. At the foot of his bed, a lunula of water has formed on the dark earthen floor.

Pilote moans softly in his sleep.

La Sierra Maestra

The afterbirth of winter is a no-season that drags on. For ages, no sun has broken through the solid pie-plate sky. As though the earth had abandoned its long looping revolutions and tight rotations. Time frozen somewhere in the dingy alley between day and night. Even the birds have gone to seed in their mangy nests, picking at the filthy lice in their feathers and repeating the same three-note whistle as though a kind of tape-loop had been installed in the treetops.

Ché scrambles out of the makeshift shelter of corrugated cardboard, twigs and scraps of tin where he has been sleeping and works his way along the dirt path under the trees up to the lookout. The cobbled plaza in front of the Chalet is empty save for Clytæmnestra, standing, as usual, at her post by the edge of the stone parapet. Low on the western horizon, a dirty twenty-five watt moon hesitates between sinking out of sight and dying right there in the sky. Clytæmnestra watches the pale globe the way insomniacs in the city stare at that last point of light just before their TV screens go blank.

Ché shrugs, leaves her there on the terrace, wrestling with the moon. He slings his empty mochila over his shoulder and starts down the path. It has been a long time since he has gone down. Even now, he would prefer not to go. Better to remain high in the mountains, perched above the city. To wait. But for how long? And for what? "In the beginning we were few; now..." he mutters, breathing hard with the effort of the descent, "we are few again."

Climbing through the dense jungle for days without catching sight of anything. The gondola, the work gang carrying supplies back to the main camp. Only the sound of the machetes clearing the way and the ferns swishing back to the next man in the file. And of course his own breathing, which no one could fail to recognize: that constant, laborious wheeze. No city below, no manmade bridges and highways spanning rivers and empty space. Nothing to verify their existence, not even a target for their anger. And yet, during all that time, the sun had shone brightly, piercing the green vault of their retreat, exposing all the shit and stupidity of the world as they crashed through the forest from village to village, laughing in the face of the Divine Watchmakers' Trust, trampling the accountants, dreaming holes in the bank vaults. But all that was during the long tropical summer. Before victory. Before they entered the city. At some point—but when, exactly?— the light had faded. He remembers the celebrations, a banquet. There had been a house in the suburbs.

He draws out the empty Ventolin pump and in one smooth motion sucks in two quick shots, slips the inhaler back into his pocket, shakes his head and pauses on the path, barely whispering between long painful breaths, "The revolution is not a banquet." Allows himself the luxury of a quick chuckle, more of a truncated grunt, and resumes his walking down the slope, the late winter cold tugging at his ragged sleeves.

At the base of the mountain, he quits the park and suddenly finds himself in the midst of three lanes of traffic, looking down the steep slope of Peel Street into the core of downtown Montreal. He stands ankle-deep in the rush of spring runoff pouring down into the sewers and waits to adjust to the transfer from forest to city centre. In his ragged beret, army jacket and muddy boots, unshaven, uncombed, fingering his memories like worry beads, his head still full of empty sky and wind, Ché begins to wander aimlessly into the store-lined streets and crowds. Until suddenly he is standing at the door to the Sierra Life Insurance Company on Peel Street. This, he suddenly realizes, must be the place to which he has in fact been dragging himself— kicking and screaming—all along. He is going to beg assistance from Leche.

Before him, a wall of black glass. If only he still had his own dark glasses. Reluctantly, Ché revolves into the lobby, where he is confronted by a gigantic tree, ten or twelve feet in diameter, branches ranging high in the bubble of the glass ceiling overhead and leaves like giant olive-green kites gently waving in a light breeze, whose origin, in this self-contained environment, is a mystery. A thick orange rubber fire hose has been grafted directly into the trunk of the tropical hybrid, probably, he guesses, pumping some mysterious biochemical concoction of ultra-growing agents directly into the root system. It must be pumping very heavily, judging by the size of the plant, which seems to be sweating a thin green mist into the lobby. The fog makes it difficult to breathe.

Ché takes another double shot from his useless pump. Circles the tree. For an instant, he is overtaken by a strange temptation to scramble up onto the lower branches. Why? To gain a vantage point over the terrain? Or something else? The gentle swaying motion once you reach the upper branches. Don't look down. Not yet. Keep climbing. A few thin branches more. Now. Look down. The garden down to the Mendoza River. The wrought-iron table, the bench by the roses. And the wind. First the whistle in the trees behind the house like a warning, then the rocking and your stomach all queasy your legs turned to rubber just hold on close your eyes and wait it out until the wind passes the silence returns and the branch is still again. She's calling from the doorway, calling your name, moving into the garden, toward the water, until she comes into view down below, just at the edge of the branches, but you can barely look straight down that way without the queasiness rising up again so you wait until she has gone a ways toward the water. "Ernesto." She calls again, in that voice devoid of anger or concern. Singing it: *Er-nes-ti-to. Er-nes-ti-to.* She is wearing her bathing suit and a towel wrapped around her shoulders, and you know that, later, after you have come down and gone swimming in the cold dark water, she will wrap you in her towel, rub you warm and dry in her arms. But you're not ready to come down yet. Not until the fear has been beaten. From here you are an angel looking down from the sky, watching over her and the garden, the house and everyone in it. *Er-nes-ti-to.*

Breathing is more difficult in the mist. He circles the trunk and steps up to the bank of twelve chrome elevators along the wall. Twelve doors immediately slide open. He steps into the third elevator. Instead of floor numbers, a series of pictographs appears in a bluish light on the glass panel to his right. The use of pictures instead of numbers, Ché decides, is probably intended to spare the passengers the terrible knowledge of just how high and fast they are going. There are no buttons to press, so, being alone and, as far as he can tell, unobserved, he tries whispering, "La Sierra Maestra." When he gets no response, he extends a tentative index finger and brushes the image of a golden cliffside on the panel—the doors slide shut, the elevator whooshes skyward, his ears pop.

When the doors slide apart once again, he steps out onto the thick coal-grey carpet of what he assumes are the offices of the Sierra Maestra Life Insurance Company, although there are no signs to confirm this. His nose is running; a trickle has already reached the edge of his upper lip before he can investigate. Once on the back of his hand, the liquid appears to be watery pink blood. He forages a crumpled wad of lint and ancient newspaper from his pocket and presses it to his nose. He is light-headed. The outer office contains a few luxuriously upholstered pieces and a small mahogany desk, but no receptionist. He unslings his knapsack and starts to sit down on a beige leather sofa close by the door, intending to wait, but, before he can drop his butt onto the seat, he notices an open door to the right. Without straightening up he takes two or three steps and peeks gingerly into the open office. There, standing by a window offering a panoramic cityscape and a clear view of the mountain, is Leche himself. The beard is still there, only greyer and combed out, the face rounder, puffy around the eyes and, of course, down below, the olive-green shirt is stretched tight over a large, serious paunch. The teeth, however, have improved: somewhere along the way, his old comrade has obviously gotten hold of a whiter and straighter set than the ones Ché pulled out for him.

"Come in, come in," Leche motions, as though he's been expecting him. Ché, still bowing in a frozen first movement toward sitting, steps into the office and immediately, even before he can straighten up, freezes, dazzled by the polished steel and clear glass furnishings all around him. He can see little bits of himself reflected everywhere: his foot on the leg of the coffee table in the centre of the room, his knee on the arm of the chair toward which his host motions him, and a brown eye—either his or Leche's, he can't be sure—twisting around the corner edge of the desk. Ché stuffs his rosy tissue back into his pocket and completes, at last, the sitting manoeuvre he had begun in the waiting room.

Leche lowers himself comfortably into an oversized chair behind the desk, gently lays his muddy cigar in a bottle-green ashtray and gives Ché the once-over. The glance, although quick and casual, is sufficient to make Ché shift in his seat, which immediately sets the bits and pieces of his reflection spinning all over the room again.

"Well, you old unrepentant Trotskyite, how have you been?" Leche grins.

"They've got us pretty badly bottled up," Ché says.

Leche swings out of his chair and returns to the window. Ché can just make out a view of the cross and the mountain. It occurs to him that the camp might be visible from here, and he is about to pull himself out of his seat to get a closer look when Leche turns abruptly and, stepping up beside him, places a large hand on his shoulder.

"Strategically, we remain in a period of consolidation."

Ché shrugs. He really has no desire to engage in this tired old debate, but he knows the other expects it. "We cannot risk isolation," he recites without enthusiasm. "A revolution that ceases to expand will suffocate."

Leche steps to the side, assumes a wrestling stance and growls: "We cannot risk losing our precious foothold over a reckless adventure."

Ché, tired, does not want to play.

Leche prods him with a thick finger just beneath the collar bone. "Come on, comrade, don't give up so easily."

Ché takes a deep, difficult breath. "To survive, a fire must spread," he offers.

"Good, good," his old friend grins, "but you've got that mixed up with capitalism: the fire-spreading metaphor." He slips on the mask of an angry glare. "In the present context, surrounded and isolated," he says, his voice rising, "construction is the primary and urgent task of the permanent revolution."

"We need two, three Vietnams," Ché responds. "The international alliance of the proletariat and the oppressed peoples of the world is not, in the present context, strong enough to engage in a direct conflict with the forces of capital and reaction." In spite of himself, he can feel the words beginning to lift him off his feet. "Trench war, fixed positions, neatly delineated lines of battle: all this is suicidal. Let us light a thousand small fires behind enemy lines, in every corner of the globe, in the heart of the bastion of imperialism, everywhere, anywhere." Leche grinning ear to ear. And the words frothing, wet and hot. "The enemy should never be permitted to fix our position. To survive, the revolution must remain in constant motion, shifting, sliding, blurring the frontiers, slipping through the cracks." Keep it coming. "Not a series of direct blows at the head, but rather, quick, sharp, peripheral hits—crack a finger, snap a small toe, blunt the opponent's thinking, sap his will." Words, cascading over his head, sweeping him off his feet, now he's tumbling below the liquid surface of the sentences. She was waiting by the shore, ankle-deep at the edge of the river, waiting with the dark warm towel. To wrap him in it, rub his back, his legs, her lips close to his ear. *Ay, Teté, my little shivering frog.* A lock of her dark hair falling, falling along his back, burning ember on his pale shoulder. Whispering.

How long has he been speaking? What has he said? Leche, silent, serious, studying him with something resembling concern but which might simply be curiosity. Ché concentrates on pressing his lips tightly together. Waits for the moment to pass.

Leche, silent, frozen in his wrestler's stance. Then suddenly he roars with laughter and Ché can see all the excellent bridgework in his mouth. "At least you haven't put on weight," he says. "Look at me." He places two hands over his belly. "It's a disgrace, I know. But what can I do? I'm behind this desk all day." He is laughing, but Ché can see the eyes studying him.

"We are short of supplies," Ché says.

Leche straightens, nods and circles back behind his desk. He settles into his chair and relights his cigar. "I may have something for you," he says. "Lately we've been selling a lot of group policies to trade unions. Big packages. The premiums are not great but the quantities make up for it. Only problem is, the disability claims are killing us. We can't drop the coverage; they won't buy the package without disability."

Ché feels weak and tired. The window is to his left. If he rose and walked over, the entire face of Mount Royal would be in clear view. Could he spot the camp from here? He will have to do something about that. Those shower curtains they are using for roofing are too colourful. Transparent plastic sheeting would be better, but it's difficult to come by—nobody throws it out—and rarely thick enough to withstand the weather.

Leche is talking about the insurance business. "No one is going to tell me those cases are airtight," he argues, slamming his hand down on the desk. "I'd guess sixty percent of them have got something on the side. Odd jobs, a cousin needs some repairs on the house, a brother owns a small business, a few hours here, a few bucks under the table there. Who can blame them? Except it's in the contract. Disabled. Disabled is defined as unable to work…"

Ché's mind keeps dipping in and out of the conversation. Occasionally he manages to get a handhold but almost immediately it slips out of his grasp and he is drifting slowly down again below the surface of his old comrade's voice.

"…some serious investigating. Of course, it involves a bit of legwork…"

Suddenly Ché realizes he is being offered a job. The idea is so absurd he almost bursts out laughing. His tongue is already polishing the phrases of polite refusal when something stops him. Perhaps he ought to simply get up and walk out. After all, this is a kind of insult, isn't it? Yet, he's still seated, his face arranged in an attitude of listening. What is he waiting for? For the man in whose body he is lodged to shout, get up and move. Or maybe, it's just cunning: he's playing out line, letting the fish run. Checking out the possibilities. There might be something in it for the revolution. But no, this is a job. Doing someone's dirty laundry, washing the blood out of their clothes, covering their tracks, oiling the machine, stoking the furnaces. For a moment, he imagines himself taking a bus into work in the early dawn, filing through the gates, the warm press of bodies all around, the grip and punch of the clock on his heart. The idea of working nine to five, even if just for a few days, seems like a vacation. Not to have to think ahead or analyze. No strategic considerations, no waiting and watching for the enemy. And, at the end of the week: a paycheque… The essential thing for the guerrilla, after all, is not to let himself be destroyed. Meanwhile, Leche has been chattering away, something about talking to neighbours, photographs…spying.

Hermeneutic Circle

They start him in Claims. A vast unbroken space stretching over an entire floor of the building, either several floors above Leche's office or a hundred stories underground, no way of telling from the elevator ride, and there are no windows, only this huge room filled with clusters of small desks, grouped together in fours and separated by thin temporary panels. If the ceiling were not so low and the employees had the time and means to climb to a great height, their workplace would look from there like an endless field of clover. But that vantage point is not available. The long wide garden leading down to the water and the wind in the branches all around him, the gentle swaying. Now she's passing directly below, one hand on her sun hat, her long light skirt swaying as she walks toward the shore, the meandering step, an occasional skip, the way someone walks when she thinks she is alone. Each desk is equipped with a computer terminal and a claims assessor. Every hour on the hour, a plague of clerks descends upon the clusters of keyboarders, leaving piles of dental and medical claims in its wake. Ché's job, and that of all his co-workers, is to transfer the information on these forms into data on his screen. As a result of his labours, he imagines, somewhere at the end of the network, in some place he will never see, a super-printer spewing a neverending stream of signed and sealed cheques directly into the postal system.

The work is not entirely routine. He is not to pay without a struggle. His job consists mainly of finding ways to reject the claims, to cut off benefits. Dates, eligibility of drugs, treatments, maximums, deductibles: everything has to be checked. At first Ché is happy in his work. The simple drudgery acts as a kind of therapy after years of improvisation and skin-of-your-teeth survival. Aside from the clicking of the keyboards and shuffling of paper, the room is quiet. No time for chitchat or personality conflicts; they are all on quotas.

And he's good at it. His paycheques he cashes and stuffs into his socks. The money will go to the cause. To maintain security he has adopted the name Ramón Benítez Fernández, an identity for which he still has a passport—an excellent forgery, albeit expired. Now that the attendants know him, he can usually spend the nights in the garage of the building or wander the underground mall.

In spite of his unusual hygienic and vestiary habits, he appears to be fitting in. Soon they are giving him the tougher claims, the short-term disabilities; this requires reading accident reports, doctors' evaluations, medical textbooks. The pressure to reject claims is mounting. The work becomes less routine. In some ways it is more like problem-solving—digging up hidden clauses in the contract, contradictions in the report, decoding doctors' diagnoses, excavating historical precedents. There is also a philo-sophical component—contemplating the relativity of pain thresholds, pondering the nature of work as fundamental human activity or necessary evil, juggling the dialectics of human and corporate responsibility, distin-guishing accident from act of God.

This combination of archaeology and metaphysics troubles Ché/Ramón. Also, as the amounts of money involved grow, so do the consequences of mistakes, and his responsibility toward the Company. Worse, until now he has not really thought about the insured themselves; he begins to get a clearer picture of the faces behind the forms: the wounded industrial labourer, the burned-out white-collar worker. He imagines their dismay, frustration, despair, as they receive his demands for further clarification and additional humiliating and painful visits with the Sierra medical staff. Occasionally he catches a glimpse of the enemy in his own reflection. The dank smell of the dungeons of La Cabaña fills his nostrils. The parédon. Revolutionary justice? Reign of terror? In the case of that butcher Castaño Quevedo, it was a pleasure to give the order. How many men had Castaño's Bureau for the Repression of Communist Activities sent to their deaths? For Castaño, Ché would have pulled the trigger himself. Those who followed immediately after were all pigs. Hands dripping blood. When he felt his will flagging he stirred memories: the traitors, those who had tried to profit, to take advantage, to murder in the dark of night. Eutimio Guerra. He thought of those who had fallen: Juventino Alarcón, Pastor, Yayo, Castillo, Oliva, Julito

Díaz. Little Vaquerito, the barefoot cowboy. And Julio Zenón Acosta, Ché's first pupil in the Sierra. Julio, illiterate guajiro, forty-five years old, in his quiet determined way working tirelessly, perfectly adapted to the hard life that drove so many recruits back down to the plains. A fish in the Sierra sea. Julio, who knew the area, knew how to live in the forest. It was Julio who showed the city boys how to make a quick fire, Julio who could find dry kindling on a rainy day, Julio who trekked miles to bring them water from distant and secret water holes. He had decided to learn to read. After the revolution, he told Ché, there would be enormous tasks. It was early February. That week they had started on the vowels. But then Eutimio Guerra, with whom Fidel had shared his own blanket only days earlier. His mother was sick, he told them. And Fidel gave permission to visit. But Eutimio Guerra betrayed them, returned with the airplanes, led the army's ambush at Altos de Espinosa. And that's how Julio Zenón Acosta, trapped on the hillside, was cut down with no more than a handful of vowels running through his head.

Every day, pouring over the files of the accused in his small cell of an office in La Cabaña, Ché rehearsed the betrayals, squeezed tears over the dead. Within days his mouth was filled with the taste of ashes. The moment of realization, that mixture of defiance and fear, a twitch in the eye, a slight trembling of the lower lip. The uncertainty at first—surely this can't be happening to me—and then, yes, the blood draining from their faces. At first, he had given them the time to understand, to fully grasp the finality of the verdict. He had waited for that look of realization. Shared it with them. But soon he had learned to shuffle them out quickly before death registered, so that the understanding took place behind the blindfold. The worst part was the signing. All night, file after file, writing death with the quick smooth stroke of his pen. His name transformed into a death's head. And Neruda's words tap-tapping on his skull. Hatred growing scale on scale, blow on blow, in the ghastly water of the swamp, with a snoutful of slime and silence.

So, by the time he is called in for a second meeting, Ramón is already preparing his resignation speech. Unfortunately, when he walks into the room, Leche is already speaking. "Of course, you, a man of action sitting around, impersonal desk job, not for you. The open air, interactive, good with people, a born leader, out in the field...What do you say?"

A way out of the long low-ceilinged room, a step, after all, in the right direction, out into the street, back toward those hills to which he fully intends to return and the sooner the better. Of course, this is clearly not the best time to raise that issue with Leche. Too early to expect he would let him go and grant the additional supplies the camp desperately requires. And isn't that, above all else, Ramón's mission here: to rearm, refurbish the revolution? Or at least bring some relief. But too soon for that. Probably better to do his stint as this new thing Leche has been describing …this claims investigator… A couple of weeks or so and then back to the office, with a detailed proposal this time. Before dismissing him, his old comrade presents a gift, a gourd and a small sack of the best Argentine yerba maté, the same bitter tea Ernesto learned to sip on his father's farm on the pampas. "Try not to make another fracaso this time," Leche tells him gently. He is referring, of course, to Ramón's stint at the Ministry of Industry. Or does he mean the Congo adventure? Ramón puts the maté carefully away in his knapsack with the extra pair of underwear and socks he has allowed himself to purchase and the rest of the money. Outside in the hall, he pauses to write in his journal: *A new stage begins today.*

His first case is a long-term disability living in the southwest of the city by the Lachine Canal. Ramón buys a string of bus tickets, pockets the receipt for travelling expenses and takes the subway down to Lionel-Groulx station. From there, a ride on the 211 bus for another forty minutes into the industrial park. By the time he steps down, pausing to take a couple of shots from his inhaler, it is midmorning. The subject lives in a triplex on a sidestreet along the tracks between the Lachine Canal and the old Dominion Bridge plant. The river, angry and frothing brown scum. The thin hair-like weeds brushing against his legs, the mud sucking on his ankles. And she sitting on the shore, waiting with the large turquoise towel spread open and ready to receive him. The railroad tracks weave along the canal between the water and the old industrial factories. Roman ruins, blunted pyramids, the segmented columns of the Parthenon. The cold wind, as though mocking the proletarian vanguard, blows off the water, over the empty fields and the shells of abandoned factories littered with twisted cranes, rusting machine parts, a bombed-out railroad car.

As instructed, Ramón does not make himself immediately known to the subject. He begins with the neighbours. Their willingness to talk is a surprise. Still, progress, if any, is slow. What do a man's neighbours know about him? What will they tell you? You are likely to learn as much or more about them as him: their values, priorities, where they draw the line between natural idiosyncrasies and social deviance, how much time they spend watching their neighbours. About him, maybe nothing. Ramón might have done better to limit himself to one or two, because with every additional witness, the image gets murkier. A cold solitary man, suspicious, idle, a chip on his shoulder, generous to a fault, polite, handsome in a rough sort of way, good with children, a real gentleman, a brain if you know what I mean, an intellectual, all those books, a bear, not a peep out of him after ten o'clock, burning the midnight oil, a man of action, up at the crack of dawn, so little trash compared to other people, the bottles, in the house all day except for the early morning and after dinner walks, no regular hours, saw him on the back porch with a hammer, always plenty of mail, probably taking in work if you ask me, writing articles, those late night meetings… The problem here is one of hermeneutics: there seems to be no way to make the pieces fit into a clear picture.

Ramón tries the house across the way. A pensioner living alone. Born and brought up in the neighbourhood. And full of information. "Known the man for centuries, since he moved in. Such a tragedy. Life is a swine, that's my opinion. He used to stop and chat, out in front of the house, putting the garbage out, coming home from work. Knew a lot, I'll grant him that. A librarian, what do you expect? A lot of good it did him, all those books. Bang. A stroke. Dumb as a doorknob. Right in the reference section, I hear. And they put him out without a second thought. All that education. Now, he can't even tell me the time of day. As for me, I'm a student of the world. How to make ends meet. Books can't help you there. Does he go out? Sure, from time to time. Wandering around, I expect… But work, no. Absolutely not. What could he do in his condition? What good are all those books to him now?"

Turning back toward the subject's side of the street, Ramón spots a face in a third-floor window. Small sharp eyes in a puffy mask of flesh, framed in limp grey hair. It takes her some time to answer the door; she can't stand on her swollen ankles for very long so she invites him in to sit at the kitchen table. Arboreta, red-and-white checked curtains, instant coffee, the smell of cigarettes and shepherd's pie.

"Of course, he's working on the sly. Disabled, my foot. Speech impediment? Who told you that? The fellow across the way? That drunkard? I tell you, the man can speak as well as you or I. I saw him myself talking to the birds over in the parking lot, you can see it from here: that paved-over bit full of trash next to the garage. Chattering away at those lousy pigeons like some old grandmother. And feeding them, too. As though there wasn't enough garbage out there for them. Filthy birds."

"But did you actually hear him speaking to them?"

"You calling me a liar? Don't you think I can tell when someone's yammering? He was right over there, I tell you. If that man's dumb, I'm blind."

Ramón says little, simply poses the questions on his list one after the other. It would be difficult to actually engage in conversation, to speak to them. What could he say? He might rail at their lack of solidarity, their willingness to rat on a neighbour, and without so much as a reward, just for the sheer malicious pleasure. But he needs the information. He's a double agent to the nth degree: talking to these neighbours, the job itself, his relations with Leche—all on false pretenses. His own betrayals: Argentina, Cuba. And the women: first Hilda, then Aleida and the children. All for the revolution. Or Hilda for Aleida, Aleida for Tania. Even that seems hazy. He's lost track of how many levels of betrayal are involved.

The subject takes even longer to answer the door. A large soft-fleshed male with wild grey hair and unruly beard, thick glasses, worn slippers and a bathrobe. Ramón introduces himself as an encyclopaedia salesman. At first the Librarian does not seem to understand. Then he shakes his head apologetically, tries in vain to force a syllable from his throat and begins to swing the door shut. No, no, Ramón tells him. Not to sell the books. To write them. He takes advantage of the old man's confusion to slip past and into the apartment. A short dark hall leads into a combination living room–bedroom. Everything here is covered in books, papers and newspapers. He moves through into the kitchen, which is also a mess. "You mind if I sit for a moment?" He brushes away some of the crumbs scattered over the surface of the formica table, smearing his hand in a streak of peanut butter for his trouble.

The Librarian is still groaning at the door. It takes him forever to shuffle in and join his guest. Ramón can hear him wheezing with the effort.

Ramón starts in on him before he has a chance to sit down. "Recruiting experts to compose the entries in our encyclopaedia, the highest standards, international scholarship, twenty-six volumes, leather-bound, gold leaf... Your name was given to us at the University... your work on the negation of the negation, largely unrecognized until now, a renewed interest in negativity these days..."

Suddenly remembering his manners, the old man drags himself over to the stove to turn the heat on under a pot of stagnant water. He searches through the mound of dirty dishes and salvages a cup, runs it under the tap for a moment and dries it on the sleeve of his bathrobe. Then either because he has forgotten what he set out to do or simply because he is too tired to go on, he collapses in the chair across from his guest.

"Never mind," Ramón says. "I'll take care of it." Rummaging in the mostly empty cupboard for coffee or tea bags, he finds a forty-ounce bottle of vodka, already seriously broached, and two dark Cuban rums. "Ah, we could both use a bit of this." With a single glance at the sink he abandons any notion of a glass and brings a bottle of each alcohol back to the table.

He detects a spark of interest in the old man; until now he had not noticed the intelligence in the dark eyes. "What's your poison?" he asks, placing the two bottles between them. The old man turns his gaze on the Russian sentinel. Ramón pours two fingers into his host's coffee mug. The Librarian glares at the cup for a moment, shrugs and downs the contents in a single throw.

"You don't mind if I stick to my own brand?" Ramón says, refilling the old man's cup with vodka first, this time without counting fingers. "Don't shoot," he says, raising the bottle of rum for a toast. "We are worth more to you alive than dead."

Heavenly Portents

All through the night, the rain has been beating a tattoo on the plastic curtain over her head. In the early dawn, she drags her sore joints and damp heart up through the trees to the lookout. Here, for the first time in these three millennia, she receives the strange greeting of three separate suns, each crowned in a pale rainbow of shifting colours, rising out of the mist over the river. Immediately the Argosian Queen turns to look for Suzy, a witness to confirm the sign. But the girl is not there. Hasn't been around since…she can't remember. The square is empty. No one to read this message from the Gods. Only Clytæmnestra, the grey drizzle rising off the grey stones, and the three pale discs rising in the haze over the river.

Inside the fortifications at Pointe-à-Callière, Paul de Chomedey stands in three inches of water. All through the night he has been working to seal the cracks, plug every leak in the shelter, but by morning he is forced to admit that the water is not so much coming down through the roof as seeping up from the ground inside the trench.

Le Corbusier is fast asleep, jacket carefully folded beneath his head, glasses and bow-tie in a shopping bag at his feet, hands resting in plain view on his chest over the blanket of newspapers. Oblivious to the emergency. Lost in symmetrical dreams.

There is no avoiding it; the Governor will have to make his own scouting party, go out in search of boarding or tin sheeting, anything to put between them and the soaking earth. He prepares as best he can, stuffing paper into his boots, pulling his arms through a couple of plastic bags. He steps out into the rain, pausing, bare head bowed, to cross himself, offer a prayer to the Virgin and cross himself again, before starting out toward the docks where he might find some stray planks. He can hear the rush of the river through the rain. Then, through the current's roar, a strange cry, like an infant's wail. He turns in time to spot a single white porpoise clear the curled grey surface of the river. The Governor hurries down to the water's edge. Waits. Another piercing cry and a second porpoise, as white as the first, breaks the surface. And then a dozen more, leaping together, punctuate the river. White apostrophes on a grey page, opening and closing quotations. Suddenly, the seaway is filled with a hundred, a thousand leaping porpoises, all pure white and wailing. As though the river were remembering all the names of its drowned. In the cobbled street, de Maisonneuve stands, unable to move or speak, frozen in the siren's song. An eternity in an instant. And then they are gone. The street is silent, empty. Paul de Chomedey can hear his own heart pounding in his ears.

Dear Mr. Rockefeller

M. Rockefeller
Rockefeller Center
New York, New York
USA

Mon cher M. Rockefeller,

Le Corbusier, the greatest architect of Modernity, foremost city planner of our machine age, salutes you, the supreme captain of industry, finance and commerce.

Mon cher M. Rockefeller, I am writing to you today with a glorious proposal. But, perhaps, before I state my business, a few words of introduction. Of course, I would not presume to insult a man such as yourself with a lengthy presentation of Le Corbusier and his œuvre. Still, the magnitude of the project I am suggesting can perhaps be better understood when compared with one or two (a comprehensive compilation would be too lengthy here) of the realizations of your humble interlocutor. Allow me, therefore, to mention, in particular, two projects which together have opened the way to the future. With l'Unité d'habitation in Marseille, Le Corbusier has solved the problem of housing for the masses: this ferro-concrete high-rise with free façade and ribbon windows provides not merely shelter, but a healthy mental and physical environment for sixteen hundred people. A man with your imagination and vision, I have no doubt, can clearly see the possibilities.

The city of Chandigarh, on the other hand, offers a clear and concrete demonstration of the value of rational city planning. Here, at last, in what was to be the administrative capital of the Punjab, Le Corbusier was given free rein to plan an entire city down to the last detail, and without the encumbrance of a single previously standing structure. Instead: a vast, limitless plain. Try to imagine, sir: the geometrical event was, in truth, a sculpture of the intellect, a battle of space fought within the mind. Arithmetic, my dear M. Rockefeller, texturic geometrics: standing there, surveying the empty plain (only a few oxen, cows, goats, and the peasants driving them marred the clean slate), Le Corbusier laid a map of the city over the sun-scorched fields. Now in that self-same place stands Chandigarh, a grid of straight wide highways on crossed axes with the financial offices at the centre, and the giant housing units branching out in the arms of the cross. The Radio-Concentric City of Exchange: no more filth, disease, homelessness, disorganization. Against the vast sweep of plain and the distant mountain, Chandigarh asserts the lasting presence of man, countering the uncertainty of fate with a certainty of vision.

Planned cities, mass housing, M. Rockefeller. That is the future. But these are not possible, not on the worldwide scale which is required, without mass prefabrication of the basic components required for construction. The brilliant example of l'Unité, the perfect symmetry and organization of Chandigarh, remain models. Only when we can produce standard materials throughout the globe will mankind achieve the promise of Chandigarh and Marseille. To do this, two things are necessary. The first, concentrated financial and industrial conglomerates on a global scale, which you, M. Rockefeller, can provide. Today Le Corbusier is prepared to offer you the second.

Indeed, M. Rockefeller, today is an historic day. On this day, Le Corbusier offers you neither monument nor metropolis, but a simple ribbon. A simple ribbon of varnished cardboard, marked from 0 to 2,164 metres. This is Modulor, the universal standard of measurement. For centuries man has been divided by conflicting standards of measurement: the inch–foot, the metre, the tatami...with no single system managing to establish hegemony. And why not? Because no single measurement standard has so far corresponded entirely to both the needs of man and the proportions of nature. That is why the problem cannot be resolved simply by choosing one of the existing systems. Now, following years of arduous study and research, Le Corbusier has found the solution. Now, at last, an end to the anarchy of construction, the constant struggle between that most abstract and impractical of measurements, the European metre, and the clumsy English foot. Now, at last, standardized measurement will enable prefabrication on an international scale. Modulor is that universal standard of measurement. This simple ribbon, this trifle, is Le Corbusier's greatest achievement.

Mon cher Rockefeller, perhaps you are asking yourself, why does Le Corbusier offer this secret of global significance to me? Should he not rather present himself, Modulor in hand, before the United Nations, or perhaps the international community of architects and engineers? Why does he address himself instead to a single man—granted, a man of vast accomplishment and untold accumulated wealth—but a single man nonetheless? Ah, M. Rockefeller, do not so underestimate your position in the world of men, your destiny in the grand plan of the new and rational universe.

Once Rome ruled the world. Rome's business was to conquer the world and govern it. Rome meant enterprise, progress. A host of spectacular achievements: straight and lasting roads, social order, majestic works of art, cement. Today, you, M. Rockefeller, rule the globe. You are first among the captains of industry, and the captains of industry are the philosopher-kings of our time. You are the greatest artist. All your energies are directed toward that magnificent end which is the forging of the tools of an epoch, and which is creating throughout the whole world this accumulation of the most exquisitely beautiful things in which economic law reigns supreme, and mathematical exactness is joined to daring and imagination—that is what you do. And that, to be exact, is beauty.

You have constructed fleets of ships, vessels of freedom. To you we owe the skyscrapers of New York and Chicago. When Le Corbusier stood before these modern towers, I tell you, his heart soared, he wept with joy. Tomorrow you will build ten thousand homes to house the multitude. You will prefabricate. You will standardize. Standardized classes, functions, products, building, standardized measurement. To accomplish all this, M. Rockefeller, you need Modulor. Together we shall eliminate the arbitrary, the chaotic spontaneity of your cities. Together, Rockefeller and Le Corbusier shall build the Cartesian skyscraper, the Archimedean City.

All that is now required in order to bring this global revolution to fruition is a single hour of your time, in which Le Corbusier himself shall present to you, both in theory and in practice, the Modulor, so that you might clearly confirm the truth of what has been stated here.

Je vous prie d'agréer, cher Monsieur, l'expression de mes sentiments les plus distingués,

Le Corbusier

P.S. Due to transitional circumstances, a return address and telephone number are temporarily unavailable; however, Le Corbusier is disposed to visit you in your offices precisely at 0900 hours on the fifteenth of March of this year.

The Long March

"**O**f course, I admit I may have gone overboard in rejecting material incentives, but the larger question remains, and this is what I would like you to clarify." Ramón pours the last of the vodka into the old Librarian's glass and raises his own. "Here's to the grinding bad luck of every day; the black cup we drink, our hands shaking." The two men down their shots.

"It's all very well," Ramón continues, "to know where you're going, but how to get there? Forced collectivization, public self-criticism, re-education, it's all the same problem, really. Comes down to the old debate: doesn't all this assume man's fundamental goodness?"

The Librarian shakes his head vigorously, forces a hoarse complaint from somewhere deep in his throat. He is trying to speak. To explain. But he seems to be having trouble putting words together, and there is no wind in his throat, no sound but for a faint scratching of vocal chords. "Maa… maa…maaateerial…"

Ramón leans closer, pushes the bottle to one side, hangs on every broken syllable, staring at the chapped lips and nodding encouragement as he labours to decipher the old master's message. "You realize, of course, there are those who argue you never broke with Hegelian idealism. There's the teleological nature of the whole project… Dialectics finally reduced to yet another binarism. How do you respond?"

The old man manages one more tantalizing phrase, something about the unity of opposites, or else it's about the liquor store down the street. In any case, the strain is too much and he slumps in his chair.

Ramón pours half of the remaining rum into his host's cup. Now and again, over the past few days, he's tried to get the Librarian to respond in writing to his questions. Laying the cherry-coloured diary open on the table, he coaxes the stub of a lead pencil between the old man's fingers.

But here again, the feeble scribblings are unreadable. Faint traces, broken letters. And, in the midst of the mysterious hieroglyphics, what appears to be a complex mathematical formula resembling the old equation for surplus value, but with a strange radical, k, thrown in. Perhaps a slip of the pencil. Ramón nudges the Librarian, who has shut his eyes and appears to be dozing. The old man only smears another unreadable shadow at the bottom of the page. Given time and much labour, it might be possible to make something of it all, but at first glance, and through the golden lens of Havana Club, Ramón is stymied. No way to fix a meaning with any certainty.

Sighing, he pulls himself creaking to his feet and, gathering up the empty bottle, carries it out front where the old man keeps his recycling box. Ramón lays the bottle carefully on top of the others, the original three and those he himself has fetched in successive trips to the liquor store. The sharp eyes and puffy face are back in the third-floor window across the street. Unless they never left. Watching, counting bottles, emitting an intense narrow beam of coherent disapproval down on this house, its first occupant and Ramón as well, now that he's clearly joined the Librarian's camp. "Ah," Ramón mutters, "that one has the Cara de Cerco." The deserter's face. Sergio Acuña's face as he listened to the gunfire and heart-rending cries for help coming from the other side of the hill, just before he dropped his cartridge belt and rifle and ran; the face of Armando Rodríguez, who'd been with them from the beginning, a veteran of the Granma, before he cracked under the enemy harassment at Altos de Espinosa and took off so fast he carried the Thompson machine gun for three hours before he thought to drop it; the faces of Antonio Domínguez, Léon and Camba, who deserted Ramón in Bolivia. That's the face in the window. Or is it another face, far more dangerous? The face of betrayal—Eutimio Guerra asking Fidel for permission to visit his sick mother; Leonardo Baró, sitting with the military in the market at Las Minas de Bueycito and identifying those peasants who were in touch with the guerrillas. The face of the old woman standing among her goats in the canyon at Quebrada del Yuro. He breaks away from the gaze across the street and checks the mailbox before going back inside. A single letter, addressed to the Librarian from the Sierra Maestra Insurance Company. Back in the kitchen, the two men open it together. The letter announces an end to the Librarian's benefits, claiming he has been purchasing large quantities of alcohol and entertaining. Furthermore, according to the insurer's own medical examiner, his disability is not work-related. In any case, the letter concludes, neither oral nor any other form of communication, for that matter, are essential for library work.

Ramón blames himself, swears heads will roll, rages back and forth across the room. "We'll go to the Sierra and talk directly to Leche," he tells the old man. "Believe me, I'll settle this. They don't know who they're dealing with." But the anger only provokes a bout of asthma. He leans wheezing over the table until the old Librarian gets up and helps him sit down. Ramón grins through clenched teeth at his partner. "A fine pair we are."

The long trek up to the Sierra Maestra is hell for both of them, even more so for Ramón because of the asthma. They are compelled to make numerous pauses during which Ramón writes in his journal while the old man fondles his books. But Ramón refuses to turn back. Nor will he spend another cent of the revolution's money, stashed away in his shoe, on a taxi. There is only room for one of them to sit on the bus and Ramón refuses to let the old man stand. It takes all his strength to hang on to the strap and keep from flying into other passengers.

A black day for me; I made it by sheer guts, for I am completely exhausted. Yes. Yes to the terrible heat of the jungle, yes to the sweat soaking through his fatigues, to drinking fetid water from the swamp, to dragging himself along barefoot through the mud, to the electric taste of the dried clarín leaves that offer little relief from the asthma, to the hordes of macagüera flies coming down out of the macaw trees to bite at every inch of exposed skin so that stopping to rest is unbearable. Yes to the river swollen by the rain, the current pulling him down, while he strains every ounce of muscle to keep his gun above the water, to keep the ammunition dry, reaching, stretching his free arm to grab a branch, a tuft of grass, something, anything on the other shore. Yes to the thorny branches, his bleeding hands, the sun simultaneously evaporating the river water from his clothes and soaking them again with his sweat.

At 12:00 we left under a sun that melted the stones and shortly thereafter I had a fainting spell as we reached the top of the highest hill; from then on I walked by forcing myself. Another pipe of clarín. Yes to the heat, yes to mosquitoes, the ticks, the pain in his lungs. Burning out his body for the revolution.

The Final Renaissance Man

Fifteenth day of March. Le Corbusier bends to adjust his bow-tie in the jagged fragment of mirror propped up on his cot. He puts on his tattered jacket, smoothing out the creases as best he can, and checks his fingernails. De Maisonneuve breaks off his morning devotions. Nothing irritates him more than Le Corbusier's preening. But the architect is undeterred. "Real heroes are well-groomed and absolutely controlled. They are neither unshaven, nor unkempt, nor bloodstained. I shall arrive at the chosen time, at the proper place, calm and smiling, a conqueror and not a casualty."

"Three more centimetres, overnight," the Governor announces from his knees. "There's work to be done. We'll need more wood."

"I've told you not to use those outdated measurements." Le Corbusier is not concerned with flood control this morning. He is busy rolling and wrapping, loading up his tricycle with tattered documents and diagrams, pencils, paper, a bag of tin cans, two six-packs of empty bottles and the last of his paintings.

De Maisonneuve sighs. "If you must go out there, take Pilote."

Le Corbusier casts a doubtful glance at the dog, who yawns and grumbles briefly.

"We spotted a lone savage yesterday," de Maisonneuve insists. "Could very well be an advance scout for a larger raiding party." He makes no mention of his own heroic defense of the encampment.

"Well, I suppose he can watch my things while I go inside." Le Corbusier slips a length of rope around the mutt's neck and ties him to a handlebar. Pilote circles the cart for a moment, grunting and mumbling to himself until he finds a clear spot in the back between Le Corbusier's unsold paintings and a stack of corrugated cardboard. Carefully he lifts his old bones up and makes himself comfortable. He has no intention of walking.

The sky is still overcast but the rain has let up temporarily. Full of confidence and without pausing to examine the trash bins along the way, Le Corbusier sets out along rue Saint-Paul toward University Street and the city centre. At this hour of the morning, the sidewalks are jammed with office workers, so he pushes his tricycle-cart along the gutter of the road, weaving between the parked cars and angry motorists. He ignores the horns and occasional insults, crosses boulevard René-Lévesque and parks his cart by the taxi stand on Union Street. He leaves the dog, who seems to have settled back to sleep, in charge, gathers up a handful of scrolled documents, and enters the east wing of Place Ville-Marie, slipping past the security guard dozing in front of a wall of closed circuit screens and into the elevator. As soon as he steps inside, the doors slam shut and before he can press any buttons his heart is in his throat. Almost as quickly the elevator bangs to a stop. Le Corbusier, pink-faced and flustered, steps out without checking the floor and finds himself in the underground shopping plaza. On the wall beside the elevator an arrow pointing down the hallway promises a way up to the offices. Soon he is lost in a maze of boutiques.

As far as he can tell he is still in the east block of the cruciform, but there is no way of knowing for sure. He enters a small shop to ask for directions, spots a saleslady in what turns out to be the women's lingerie section, and quickly finds himself entangled in panties and brassieres. He retreats before the saleslady's suspicious gaze, knocking over a rack of pink lacy things on his way out the door. A few hundred yards down, Le Corbusier pauses to catch his breath and check his reflection in a pyramid of analgesics behind a drugstore window. He is perspiring. "Well-groomed, controlled," he whispers at his sectioned image in the glass. "Calm and smiling." He takes a deep breath and strides purposefully toward what he believes is the centre of the complex.

He soon finds himself almost alone in a dead-end corridor. Something is happening down at the end of the row of stores. A scuffle. An elderly woman being harassed by some kind of hoodlum. Le Corbusier turns to retrace his steps, but the woman has spotted him. She calls out in a surprisingly strong voice for help. He hesitates. The assailant seems to be alone and not very tall. Head shaved, bare arms in a T-shirt, black boots.

Trying to grab the dark-haired lady's shopping bag. Then he recognizes the assailant. Well, this is too much. "Hey," he shouts, marching toward the pair.

The skinhead girl drops the old woman to the ground, turns toward him. It *is* her: that girl he ran off Place Jacques-Cartier the other morning. "Look here, young lady," Le Corbusier begins, but before he can launch into his lecture, she pushes past him and is off running down the hallway. He watches her turn the corner, then bends to help the victim to her feet. At first she is all meekness and gratitude, showering him with thanks, leaning on his shoulder, clinging to his arm. But then, she breaks off her sighing and steps back to take a good look at him. And he takes a good look, too. An old woman yes, but long dark hair — is it dyed? — and blazing eyes, in which he can't help but notice something, a glimpse of disappointment. He glances quickly into the glass of a shop window. No, nothing wrong. His jacket is badly worn, the shoes too, but the charm and style are still there. He lays his own packages down and retrieves her shopping bag, handing it over with his best smile. "Are you hurt, Madam? Shall I seek assistance?"

"No," she waves him off. "Go, go. I'm fine."

But this is almost rude. Le Corbusier tries once more. "Allow me to present myself: Le Corbusier."

Nothing.

"The architect… Ronchamp? La Maison Citrohan? The Villa Stein…"

"Yes, yes…" She waves him off again, looking down the corridor after the runaway hoodlum girl. Come to think of it, the old woman's clothes are somewhat shabby. It occurs to Le Corbusier that she could be an itinerant. Which might explain her strange behaviour: one of those psychiatric patients they've been turning loose in the streets for lack of funding. Now, while he wonders why the skinhead would bother to pick on this old woman, she puts two fingers to her lips and produces one of those piercing whistles dogs go crazy for. Immediately the hoodlum girl reappears at the end of the hall. Moves cautiously back toward them.

"Never mind," the old woman tells her. "Worst luck, he's only a beggar."

"Oh, shit," Suzy says, recognizing him, "the garbage picker down in Old Montreal."

Le Corbusier is too busy working out the scam to protest the slander. "She was not robbing you," he tells the old woman, as though she didn't know.

She ignores him, turning to the girl instead. "What's wrong with your eyes, you could not recognize him?"

"It's not the eyes," the young one says, "it's the memory. Things come and go."

The old woman shakes her head. "Now we'll have to begin all over in another spot. We've been here too long."

"He had a kind of three-wheeled bike with a cart…and all kinds of junk," Suzy says, staring at Le Corbusier. "And gears. You put those gears together yourself," she adds with grudging respect.

"A trifle. Allow me to present myself…" Once more, the architect lists his achievements, limiting himself to those projects that were actually realized.

Suzy shrugs and nods toward her companion. "Clytæmnestra's a queen."

Le Corbusier turns with a quick bow of the head and a smile to the dark woman. "Ah, Agamemnon, conqueror of Troy. You are his wife?"

"And his executioner," Clytæmnestra replies sharply, turning a heavy-lidded gaze on him.

"Daughter to Leda, sister to Helen, Queen of all Argos," Suzy recites.

"Yes," Le Corbusier effuses, "The Kingdom of Argos, the temple of Athena, the Parthenon." And immediately he's off: "The Parthenon, that terrifying machine! Une véritable sculpture au bord de l'Acropole, bathed in the intensity of the light of Attica. Ah, the genius of Phidias. Nothing like it has been done anywhere before or since. It happened at a moment when things were at their keenest, when a man, stirred by the noblest thoughts, crystallized them in a plastic work of light and shade. Infallible and implacable, the savage plain, the immaculate structure. The spirit of power triumphs. The cruel immobility of the entablature terrifies. Riveted, mentally ravished, we are in the grasp of superhuman destiny. The herald, with his terrible and piercing gaze, raises to his lips the bronze trumpet and a cry echoes. All is reduced to dust."

"C'mon," Suzy says, pulling on Clytæmnestra's sleeve. "This one's got a bad case of logorrhea."

But Clytæmnestra is thinking of the temple, the goddess Athena. She can never think of Athena without the old bitterness returning. It is not so much the judgement itself that angers her, but the very fact that a woman—even though a goddess can never entirely be a woman, and in the case of Athena, that's compounded by the fact of her being born, as Apollo so cleverly argued in Athena's court, not from a woman's womb, but directly from the head of Zeus (like some divine conjecture), but still—that, in the larger scheme of things, a woman could betray her own sex, turn her back on the ire of the Furies, on a mother's grief, and take Orestes' side.

"Like it makes a difference," Suzy says. "That temple's nothing but a mess of stones. And no sign of a goddess."

That terrible trial. Orestes, clutching at the knees of power, entwined in Athena's skirts and begging for his life. As though the stain of a mother's blood could be washed from the ground. Clytæmnestra spins loose from Suzy's grasp. *Athena, give us your judgement. Which is the greater crime? A mother slays her child's assassin; a son avenges his father's death to return the rule of men. Regicide or matricide? Choose, Athena.*

"That temple is the perfect model of technological evolution," Le Corbusier continues. "The Parthenon Spirit—clarity, precision, implacable honesty, severity, economic competition—produces the perfected machine, monument to the tragedy of the human condition struggling in a hostile universe."

Then Apollo, standing smugly luminescent before the court. "Here is the truth, see how right I am." Followed by creaking syllogisms and plodding ratiocination. And Athena, swaying in her soldier's tunic, fists full of spears, her father's daughter. Rage Furies, rage! Come now, hags, crones, sluts and spinsters, come, spit and curse and rage, you wart-faced witches, drabs, vamps, Jezebels, cunts, hellcats, dykes, sirens, bitches, call girls, B-girls, houris, odalisques and Paphians, rage on, shrews, beldams, spitfires, fishwives, battle-axes, doxies, trulls, wantons, hysteromaniacs, sisters.

"The spirit of the Parthenon is the same spirit of 'imagination and cold reason' which produced automobiles and airplanes. Plastic machinery, naked, polished steel, realized in marble with the rigour that we have learned to apply to the machine." Then picking up on a sigh from Suzy, Le Corbusier offers a knowing shake of the head and extends a finger toward the girl's shoulder, but the architect thinks better of it; the finger hesitates and interrupts its original trajectory to fall short of its target and hover uncertainly in the air between them. "You are asking yourself: What is the secret of the Parthenon? Le Corbusier has discovered the answer. Look here…" he says, trying to maintain eye contact with his audience so that they won't run off while he rummages through his diagrams and scraps of paper for the Balanos plan. "These are the original sketches of the temple done in 1923. They are perfectly accurate. I have measured the Parthenon myself. C'est fait. Every stone. Every column. Every block of marble, chaque gradin et entablement. Le Corbusier now informs the world: the proportions are exact multiples of Modulor. Modulor is the basis of measurement of Ictinos, Callicrates and Phidias! Voilà! Modulor! Modulor is the secret."

A few shoppers have begun to take notice, to pause, glance, stare at the trio, drawn perhaps by Le Corbusier's rising voice, or by Clytæmnestra, who has already begun a slow spin between the shop windows. Suzy turns on the logomaniac. "Can't you shut up for one damned second? Look what you're doing to her."

"I was merely…" Le Corbusier breaks off and gapes at Clytæmnestra. "What's the matter with her?"

"Shut up," Suzy barks. If she can only keep him silent for a few moments, it might not be too late for Clytæmnestra to pull out of it. She presses two fingers on Le Corbusier's mouth and waits. In the quiet, the spinning begins to slow, like the end of a merry-go-round, one more circle, once more around, her back to them, turning and now, suddenly, face to face with Le Corbusier, completely awake and razor sharp, her eyes gleaming.

"Why," she asks, "must men be forever measuring?"

"To see whose toy is longer," Suzy chimes in, relieved.

Le Corbusier straightens. "Without Le Corbusier, there would be no great skyscrapers, none of the underground malls, the self-contained complexes in which you manage your livelihood, such as it is."

Clytæmnestra offers him a thin smile. "Pity there's no place to rest the genius's old bones within the fortress of his own design."

"I am not without resources. I have my Modulor…and an appointment."

"And a magical thinking disorder," says Suzy.

"And we've work to do," Clytæmnestra says, walking up the corridor and round the corner with Suzy in her wake.

Le Corbusier retrieves his belongings and hurries after them. "Perhaps you could direct me…" he calls after them. "The executive offices. I seem to have taken a wrong turn…" But by the time he reaches the end of the row they've disappeared in the labyrinth of shops.

He stops, stands there staring into the window displays, and completes, but without feeling, the end of his interrupted soliloquy: "Today, Modulor once again makes the inexorable precision of the Greek temple possible, pure expression of power and potency. Modulor is sublime." He mutters his way onto the long escalator leading down into the central train station. "Le Corbusier is the final renaissance."

Mermelade y Sangre

In the dream that jolts him from sleep he is floating face down, below the surface of the sea, cocooned in a thick solution of marmalade and blood when, out of the black depths, the open mouth, all teeth and throat, of a moray comes shooting up at him. He swings an arm forward in self-defense but the resistance of the water slows the motion, turning his hand into an easy target, and now the eel has gotten hold of his fist and is sucking it in, swallowing his arm right up to the elbow. He awakens before the monster can pull him into the darkness.

At first he remains motionless, waiting for dream and wakefulness to sort themselves out. He is lying on his stomach with the arm in question dangling over the side of the pallet. Then with sudden clarity he realizes his hand is immersed in liquid. He lets out an involuntary cry and, in a single instinctive motion, yanks the arm out and leaps to his feet, only to find himself standing calf-deep in a dark brown suspension of sewage. The dam is broached, the trench is filling fast. He grabs his few belongings and drabbles his way out to higher ground.

Outside, the sky is pouring down in a shower of long nails. Dazed, he turns to see the swollen river crashing over the embankment. Already a sheen of water washes over the cobbled streets. The city, his mission, Montréal is drowning. The darkness, his soul, soaked and beaten. Has God chosen to flood his fragile enterprise before it can take root? No, this river of blood and fire must surely be the devil's work. A fit of coughing brings him to his knees. Without attempting to rise, de Maisonneuve turns his face full into the teeth of the rain.

O radiant Queen of virgins, unstained, immaculate, undefiled, incorrupt, and chaste, O lily white Daughter of God, purest of roses, most blessed among women, O cloistered garden, O sealed fountain, O narrow womb of eternal truth, O resplendent paradise of grace, O glorious, fair and brilliant star, brilliant doorway of light, glistening gate of heaven, tender, sweet-scented, soft dewy petal of praise, burning bush of sinless passion, fruit of all our joy, flower of love and fount of sacred delights, O darling Mary Mother of the world, sweet Lady in Heaven, holy Virgin Mary Mother of God, hear my solemn oath: let the waters subside, return the river to its banks, and as did Your Son, our Lord Jesus Christ at Calvary, so shall I carry His cross upon my shoulders up through the tangled forest of this savage island, through a rain of flaming arrows to the summit of the mountain.

The crucifix itself is a jumble of metal, plastic, wood and glass, patched together with wire and rope: tin tubing from an oil furnace, half a car fender and a strip of blown tire, slices of broken window pane, brown-leafed branches scavenged from a dying maple, busted bits of a recycling bin, the jagged pole of a stop sign... Standing straight up, it measures almost a metre across and more than two metres high, but de Maisonneuve will be resting the crossbeam on his shoulder and dragging the long stem behind.

As he placed the weight of the cross upon his shoulders, M. de Chomedey ceased for that instant to be a mere layman. With his dark clothing, the severe cut of his hair, he seemed to us to have been transformed into a religious brother, a minister of God charged with the leadership of the faithful. Thus, long ago, Moses, Jehovah's chosen one, had become the only hope of the Israelites in the midst of the desert.

He inches forward, bent beneath his burden, across Saint-Paul and north along Saint-Sulpice toward the centre of the city, sorry now he lent the dog to Le Corbusier, because Pilote could have warned him of Indians. But he is not afraid. Oh, he's heard the talk: the Governor's lost his nerve, more piety than courage, cowering within the fortifications while the Iroquois warriors whoop and taunt from the edge of the forest and the young men of the mission chafe at the bit, itching for a fight, begging for a sortie, just a quick raid to do some damage...a taste of blood. But he cannot permit idle gossip to dictate his conduct; his first responsibility is to the mission. They are too few to risk a single casualty, and for what? Revenge? To erase their humiliation? In response to savage contempt? To satisfy the frustrations of hot-headed youth full of cooped-up energy? Pride, nothing but puffed-up soldiers' pride. No, the mission must come first, and the mission's first obligation now, in view of the temporary failure to win converts, is to survive. All the spurious talk about his so-called cowardice is nothing to him: young cocks crowing. He has nothing to prove.

Still, the talk continues, the situation worsens: there has been brawling among the men. He's weighed the options carefully. At least, at the time, it seemed to him that was what he was doing. Morale had to be considered: the doubts about his leadership, the frustrations of the young men; these, if they were left to fester, could undermine the mission as severely as loss of life. Finally, during the early morning patrol, Pilote howling and pointing; a war party was out there. Was it the crisis of morale that motivated his decision? Or pride? Always that despicable, insidious sin of pride.

Or something else. What? What was out there, beyond the palisades? Beyond the parameters of his mission? What voices that frightened him because they were unlike the voices he had heard all his life? Voices outside his mission, outside the Church. Only the wind. Strange wind in a strange land. A whispering prayer, almost inaudible, but somehow drowning out his own prayers to the Virgin. *Kontírio, Otsi'tén':'a, Ohonte'hshon:'a, Okwire'shon:'a. The animals, the birds, the green plants that heal and feed us, and the trees of the forest. Ratiwe:rahs. The Thunder Grandfathers charged by the Creator to put fresh water in the rivers and lakes.* And the water. *Kahnekaronnion.* Always the whispering prayer calling down more water. *Kahnekaronnion.* Drowning out his own prayers.

O, Madonna, Mistress, victorious Queen, redemption's fountainhead, O, immaculate Virgin, the moon and a serpent at Your feet, Virgin of the Sorrows, Your heart pierced by the seven daggers of my seven sins...

Kahnekaronnion. Kahnekaronnion...

He is moving, under his cross and the rain, up the east side of the church, so that, in a moment, as soon as he squeezes against the wall to let pass the horse and buggy and its cargo of gaping tourists beneath black umbrellas, he will turn the corner and the broad stone façade of la Basilique Notre-Dame will be there, the long low steps sweeping up to the golden portals, and high overhead, the gallery of apostles radiating all the power of Christ's love down upon his city, warming his back, lightening his load as he climbs under their protection through the streets toward the mountain. Already he can feel the surge of light and music filling his body. As though something glorious were about to happen: as though the rain were about to cease and the faithful come pouring out of the cathedral to take up their places in a long procession of fervent devotion behind him. But before he can turn the corner, his foot slips in a fresh mound of beige horse shit and slides out from under him. He goes down face first against the wet paving stones and has to lie there for several minutes, wracked by coughing and bleeding slightly from the nose. Luckily his fall has gone unnoticed. The church, its doors shut tight, appears to be empty.

He pulls himself up, heaves the great crucifix up onto his shoulder once again, and shuffles across the street to the Place d'Armes. Here, he thought he might draw some strength from the sight of the statue. His young striding figure, the wind-blown hat…but no, instead, the sight of Jeanne Mance kneeling at the southwest corner of the monument, her arm wrapped around a ragged child to whom she provides patient instruction, her face full of true selflessness, so different from his own forced humility which he has to constantly wring, one drop at a time, from the stiff canvas of his heart. If he could, he would tear that monument down: dear Jeanne, faithful Closse and Pilote to the southeast, Le Moyne and the Iroquois to the north, the frescoes, the phrases, the vain feathered Governor above, shatter all of it into dust.

March 30. They were a group of thirty. And why choose to lead the party himself? Why not send young Lambert Closse? After all, no one expected the Governor himself to go. At first, unable to find the path, over-grown with roots and fallen rocks, they are lost in patches of deep snow. Complete silence surrounds them: none of the usual birdsong or rustle of small animals; only the breathing of the men and Pilote's half snort half cough as his snout shovels through the snowbanks. But the Iroquois are out there; he can sense them, waiting in the woods all around. Slowly, painstakingly, he moves deeper into the trees. And then, at last, the first hoot and the savages are coming at them from all sides. Mohawk, a large number and wearing snowshoes, while he and his troop are rooted knee-deep in the snow, outnumbered and short of ammunition. In spite of that, his men have begun to fire wildly, pouring the crackle of wasted gunfire into the forest. And they are falling, his soldiers, his men, one by one, Matternale and Bigot dead, Guillaume Lebeau mortally wounded. Retreat. Sound the retreat. (Did he wait too long?—the sin of pride.) He takes up the rear as they begin to drag their wounded back toward the beaten track before the city gates. Step by step, in orderly retreat, until...until the fort is within sight, and the men are running, scrambling past one another, racing pell-mell for the gates. At the top of the wall, staring wide-eyed down at them: the cannoneer's eyes and the third eye, the eye of the cannon itself, pointing straight at the road full of screaming men in flight. No! Wait! But he fires. De Maisonneuve braces himself for the blow; it does not come. The cannon has misfired. His men are pouring into the gates. He turns to face the enemy, alone now except for his two pistols and Pilote hissing like a cornered cat. Is this what he had hoped for all along? Isn't the image of the men on the barricades watching him alone at the mercy of the enemy crossing his mind at this very moment? The Iroquois have stopped short, five, maybe six metres away; their chief moves forward to claim their prisoner. He stands before him, slightly taller than de Maisonneuve, wearing a French captain's jacket over his buckskins, half his face painted blood red. His eyes are dark and proud and full of intelligence and he steps forward, a hand outstretched in a kind of formal gesture, as though to receive the Governor's surrender. De Maisonneuve fires. But the chief has ducked and now prepares to leap. De Maisonneuve fires his second pistol. Pilote barking. And the other man...the other man, the shell of his face broken wide open by surprise and incomprehension...the other man falling. The bullet has pierced his skull. He has not had time to shut his eyes for death. The warriors, stunned, pause to gather up their leader and, in their moment of horrible realization, de Maisonneuve turns and flees to safety within the fortifications. Inside, cheering and the press of bodies, hands reaching out to clap him on the back, brush his arms. Hero. Single-handed, pistol-packing hero. L'exploit de la Place d'Armes. He has solved the morale problem, and wasn't that the objective of the exercise? Three of his men dead. And the other. The dark eyes full of intelligence and strength, the hand outstretched.

The light at Saint-François-Xavier turns green. De Maisonneuve adjusts the weight of the cross on his shoulder and steps off the curb. Step by painful step, the sword of rain beating on his shoulders, he turns toward St. James Street and the old financial district. He is not afraid. Still, he would have preferred to have the dog along.

Le printemps rue Saint-Denis

Sun. There must be sun at least once during the story. So sun all along rue Saint-Denis. And a perfect blue sky. A freak presage of spring, no, not even spring, summer. Although both sides of the street are bathed in the late morning light, it is the east side, the side that will remain in sun all afternoon, lined with café terraces, the side which is full of people, all the way from l'UQAM on boulevard de Maisonneuve up the steep slope to Sherbrooke, past le carré Saint-Louis and on as far as rue Saint-Joseph, people crammed together so tightly as though they were in line to get in somewhere except that the line itself is the event, people you haven't seen for a season and a half, everyone emerging from winter hibernation retrouvailles the café terraces all full fashion show la Brûlerie five hundred grams of Kenya AA en grains Gilbert Boyer the quiet sculptor outside Le Pain Doré sunglasses faces turned to the sun soaking in rays croque monsieur un allongé sans sucre un peu de crème everyone dressed casually to the aces so clever so cool isn't that the actor in Arcand's last film he's so much shorter…and outside the liquor commission on the corner of Duluth Suzy Creamcheez begging just a hand extended but wearing a worn-out woollen glove with the fingers cut off the nineteenth-century poorhouse look standing by the door to catch them coming out with an armful of bottled guilt.

Business is good. People are eager to spare some change. Every once in a while she has to scare off one of the old bums trying to horn in, but she's made five bucks already and it's not even noon. Of course, the old stinker claims it's always been his spot, and that could be, but for all she knows it might actually be hers and she forgot about it until today when it suddenly came back to her walking down Duluth from the Mountain and spotting the crowd all the way from just past Saint-Laurent. Anyway he stinks and now he's seen her shiv the spot is hers, she doesn't even have to smile at them, the assholes.

The trouble with good things is not so much that they don't last forever; it's the way they get cut short before you have a chance to remind yourself they aren't going to last forever. A police cruiser slows, comes to a halt double-parked a couple of car lengths past her. At first no action. They're talking it over. Either that or getting their nightsticks ready. Suzy checks her escape route, spots a couple of plainclothes coming up through the throng on the south side of Duluth. Once across they'll block any chance at a quick dash round the corner. The cruiser doors swing open. So it's the nightsticks. The plainclothes have moved faster than she expected, they're in the street, too late to take the corner route and the uniforms have got the north covered. Somehow the light in the sky has changed, gotten darker. Yet there are no clouds. Standing across the street in the doorway of the greasy french-fries and hot-dog joint that's been there forever, that bum she tossed, watching. Scumsucking bastard. The pincer of uniforms and plainclothes is about to close. She launches herself straight toward the bum across Saint-Denis, out between the parked cars and into the four lanes of traffic. The first driver jolts to a stop, slamming his hand down on the horn and leaving it there while Suzy springs up off his front bumper, kicks off the hood of a slowing Volvo 850 Turbo in the second lane, darts past a screeching minivan going the other way and a green Honda Civic CX with its turn signal on only to slam right into the side of an Italian twelve-speed racing bike flying to make the light. The four cops are still standing on the east side. Out in the street a municipal garbage truck has bumped the Volvo from behind ($3000 worth of damage and six days in the garage, not counting the weekend). The cyclist is down, bloody and bruised, between parked cars, his Italian racer now a mangled appendage of a pizza delivery van. But, because he has done his part for this story, cushioning Suzy's fall so that she is basically unhurt except for an ugly scrape on her chin and all her coins ripped out of the pocket of her jeans and scattered over the street, let's give the boy a helmet and, shall we say, no more than a broken collar-bone and a month in the hospital but no permanent damage. The bum, on the other hand, is nowhere to be seen.

A glance back at the cops and she's running west on Duluth, penniless, but with a mouthful of adrenaline. Meanwhile the light is funny. There's a shade edging across the sun. She cuts left on Hôtel-de-Ville to lose the pigs, skips over a little white dog—the dog barks twice sharply and his dark-haired mistress, coming down the steps from her flat on the second floor, says, "Tais-toi, Paradoxe"—swings right on Napoléon still running hard, left down treeless Coloniale, leaving les Bains Coloniale behind her, fleeing wildly now without thinking cutting back east for a couple of blocks on Roy to Laval dodging through more traffic across l'avenue des Pins to Prince Arthur the cobblestones and restaurant terraces and a sudden halt face to face with Lady Macbeth.

"The heavens," Lady Macbeth announces, removing her harmonica from her mouth, "speak to us."

Noon. Above them, the eclipse is total. The wind drops to nothing, the birds are dumb, all the colour drains from the street. The earth, its engines cut, drifts silently through space.

Black Moon Tattoo

A sudden perfect stillness. Not a bird moving across the sky, not a ripple on the river, not a breath of wind, not the slightest rustle of a leaf or blade of grass or discarded candy wrapper. In the streets and among the skyscrapers, in the trees. Nothing. The city in still life at her feet, frozen in perfect alignment with the moon and sun. A moment's pause in the slow unwinding clock of history. The river Aulis, halted in its bloody race to the sea, lies flat and colourless as granite. Even Clytæmnestra has ceased her spinning, holds her breath, stares unblinking down at the river's edge.

The moon's shadow on de Maisonneuve's upturned face. A Hail Mary pausing in its skyward journey to hover just above the mountain lookout.

The iguana, having halted its slow procession from eon to eon, squats stone-still and diamond-eyed in the midst of the path. And glaring down at Ché from the mouth of the canyon, the old woman, standing amid her silent split-hoofed goats. Nothing moves in Quebrada del Yuro.

In the underground corridors of Place Ville-Marie, it is as though they have all been buried alive, figures frozen in some future archaeological memory. Le Corbusier standing at the crossroads, his thin tidy form among the mannequins in the window of the women's lingerie shop.

Her candlelight dying suddenly, as though the air had ceased to feed the flame, as though the laws of chemistry and physics had been suspended. The candle's flicker gone. The stillness in the chamber. Even the old man's blood no longer flowing, a dark glassy pool.

Ahsonthénhkha Karáhkwa. Our grandmother the moon, source of all life, her arms wrapped around our elder brother the sun…Shonkwahtsi'a Tiehkehnehkha Karáhkwa.

The eleventh hour of his eleventh month in the Bolivian jungle.

And her mind completely blank. No memory of ever having been a child, or anything at all other than what she is at this very instant, standing breathless and cold a block west of le carré Saint-Louis, beneath the black midday moon of Montreal.

As though, in this cessation of all movement, Orestes too were no longer coming, no longer out there moving toward her, his inexorable return suspended, so that they and the city were free to live like this, a hundred centuries in peace.

A perfect symmetrical alignment. Eight hundred metres from the Louvre to the Place de la Concorde. Eight hundred metres from Place de la Concorde to Place Clemenceau. And, straight through the axis of Place de la Concorde, eight hundred metres from the Madeleine to la Chambre des députés.

His own distorted image curved across the surface of the eye of the iguana.

The damp fog of silence smothering the city.

The fur on this one's neck standing straight up, the urge to howl caught and stifled somewhere in the throat just as it was about to break loose into the air.

The goats' heads bent but not grazing, outlined black on black against the sky.

Her Iphigenia, lifeless and floating on a windless sea.

The beauty of a woman's form, the cello, the canoe, the electric turbine.

She said: *I work alone.* A phrase repeating over and over in your head.

The sun drowning in its own blood.

Behind him, the cluster of adobe huts where they had been ambushed barely a fortnight ago, La Higuera waiting patiently for his return.

The Trojans waiting on the ramparts. Agamemnon crouching silently in the belly of the horse. Iphigenia at the foot of the altar. Orestes at the gates. All frozen. Waiting.

The old woman.

A passing glance in the polished mirror of a bank window: the shock of seeing his own face after so many years, but not his face; a face full of intelligence and strength. The face of the one whose name must not be spoken.

Negation of the negation.

The trees of Birnham Wood, already leaning toward the castle.

Muggers and rapists frozen in the park.

What matters is this: emptied space. Lonely world. River's mouth.

Floating, encased in the miasma of the river.

He stood alone on the edge of the vast, empty plain. He would have to decide. Chandigarh. Not a city of lords, princes or kings confined within walls, crowded in by neighbours. It was a matter of occupying a plain. A limitless ground. A geometrical event, a sculpture of the intellect. Arithmetic, texturics, geometrics: it would all be there when he was done. For the moment, oxen, cows and goats, driven by peasants, crossed the sun-scorched fields.

O, Mother of Roman games and Greek delights...

Jeanne's face, pure, pale, the moment before she refused him.

How long had he been alone with the pain from his wounds and his burning lungs? At last his executioner, Sergeant Mario Terán, standing in the doorway with the M2 carbine. Tell my wife that she should remarry.

The Iroquois always out there waiting.

O, Mother of all living things. O, Whale of all the skies.

Her legs bent beneath her, a towel wrapped round her shoulders. Calling, *Teté, Teté*.

O, Black Moon, Black Moon tattooed across my heart.

Blood and Sand

La Catherine just east of The Main. How did we end up back here again? She remembers the sun. And running. That makes sense, because I'm breathing as though she's been running, but no sun now, just black clouds and the air like wet dog fur. That mutt down in the Old Port. Barking at me. And hungry. Mom's home cooking: apple pie, steak and potatoes. Right. Sure. More like kale and hash. Get dressed or get the hell out of the kitchen, you slut. Barking like a bicycle. Well, if we're down here, porn city, might as well try and make some coin, not that I hold out much hope, what with the cops and the pimps, plus you have to stay out of the way of the spandex girls, they pretty well have the corner to themselves. And would she miss me? If they caught me? If they picked me up, would she... Her eyelids when she sleeps. Two pale hearts beating. Perfect planets. You can watch someone dreaming. What's left for us? A bit of pavement outside the leather handbags. Leather. Black. Not the soft dull kind. Shiny. Stiff, so the edges chafe your skin. And brand new, steaming: the smell of fresh horse shit. But not handbags, for Christ's sake, people don't want nose rings and tattoos around their handbags. You'd do better outside the tattoo parlour, what with your look, or the lousy Dunkin' Donuts for shit's sake. But the girls have got the tattoos and the cops don't like anyone working that close to their doughnuts. I'd let my hair grow back, would she like that better? Hers, so long, so black. I love your hair. If I had hair like that...when she lets me brush it. Her eyelids when she sleeps...don't even think about it. Stay away from hope. Hope is a pimp. Just keep your eyes open, watch out for the cops. And the girls. Some girl with a stiletto heel. The thing is I swear I wouldn't touch. But why should she let me? Just a dumb punk. A queen works alone. Queen of cruelty, Madwoman, Mother of memories. Just to watch her when she sleeps, breathe the perfume of her blood, inhale the drug of forgetting and cross the green river, her feet asleep in my hands. Probably, this is all a waste of time. Unless some dumb het looking for a bit of S&M... If I had some leather. Or a costume, like Rudy, stepping out of the fucking peep show for shit's sake, in that fancy gaucho outfit, the fluffy white shirt, the big studded belt over the black baggy pants like a skirt, and the shining black boots, with spurs, naturally, and that hat. Jesus, that flying saucer of a hat. Fucking Rudy, looking around to make sure no one's seen him coming out of the dirty pictures, checking his patent-leather hair, then his fly. Slipping the hat on. With his stack of glossy eight-by-tens: Rudy in profile, full face, bust and full figure and, on the back, height, complexion, experience. Like some Hollywood producer would actually come down here for a quick dip.

We like Rudy. Sure, his act is a bit of a riot. And you have to watch his temper. Touchy but never fresh. That's what they say about Rudy. Always a gentleman. Even when he's down on his luck (and when is Rudy not down on his luck?) and even with her — no cracks, no dyke jokes, not like the others who treat her like I'm some kind of ET. Not Rudy. Always the famous smile, all teeth and old-world charm, and his secondhand English, right out of a phrase book. "Good day to you, Miss Creamcheez. A pleasure to see you this afternoon. We must have tea next week, yes?" and slipping into his slightly better French: "Un thé dansant chez Maxime. Ou bien le Moulin Rouge, si vous préférez." Offers one of his English cigarettes, with the monogram *RV* in gold. Where does he get them? Close up we can see the dark lines under his eyes, the thin white scar on the right cheek, pasty skin under the powder. Too much lipstick. That's Rudy, working hard to keep the show on the road.

"How's business, Rudy?"

He makes a face. Doesn't like to talk about it. Gentleman dancer, Rudy, professional host, small white button on his lapel. Not some gigolo or hustler. Not some Lounge Lizard. Like there was something wrong with that. Like bussing tables in Giolitto's or taking dictation for some cigar in a suit was better. Or making googoo eyes so they can plaster you all over the big screen. But that's Rudy. The King of Romance. Lights her cigarette with a gold-plated lighter. A flash of the platinum slave bracelet. A gift from Natasha. Turns his head to follow some john cruising down the street.

Is it the john or the Cadillac? With Rudy you never know. Likes cars, Rudy does. Once owned eight of them, if you believe him, including the famed Voisin open touring car with steel-grey coachwork, vivid red leather upholstery and the cobra embossed on the radiator cap. Big spender, Rudy. Even when he's broke (and when is Rudy not broke?). And not a stingy bone in his body. Give you the shirt off his…but never mind that. Keep your shirt on, Rudy.

On his way to pick up the mail. There'll be none. There never is. Nothing from Natasha. Nothing from Ullman. George, the Manager. The Organizer. The tango tour, $7000 a week dancing for face powders and beauty clay. With Natasha. Stepping off the boat in Montreal. The crowds. How they loved his French. And the tango finale. Not like the first time he set foot on the quay at New York, homeless immigrant, lousy wop. Any day now, he expects a letter from Ullman. From Natasha. Monday to Friday, Rudy goes by general delivery. "It is something to do, no?" He smiles. That smile again. "Something to look forward to."

Hope is a pimp, Rudy.

"I am immune to disappointment. I have even developed something of a taste for the bitter root."

The Cadillac comes around again. So not a john after all. A local pimp. And an asshole. Leans out of the car. "Hey, pretty boy."

Oh, shit. Lousy pimp. They do it on purpose. Just for a laugh. Suzy makes a grab for Rudy's sleeve, but he's already in the street, going after the car and stripping off his shirt.

The pimp keeps calling: "Come on, powder puff."

The traffic backs up at the light and Rudy whacks his palm down on the trunk of the Cadillac. The asshole doesn't like that. He steps out of the car. "Don't touch the car, fairy."

Rudy stands there, barechested: "Come, we'll see who is the real man."

Now the whores jump in. "Pretty little Rudy." They know what it does to him. Like pushing a button. Hooting and whistling. "Beautiful gardener's boy."

Rudy turns on them, then back to the asshole. He's not sure which way to go. Like teasing a cat with a string. Suzy steps in front of him. "Never mind, Rudy. Let's go pick up the mail."

Too late. Can't hear her. Gone all buggy-eyed, big close-up. Baring his chest. "Is this the body of a powder puff?" And whacking the trunk again.

The asshole moves away from the door, showing them the tire iron in his hand. "I told you not to touch the car."

Rudy assumes the correct position à la Marquis de Queensbury rules.

"Pretty boy. Pretty little Rudy." The whores. And then they see the tire iron and they stop singing. "Aw, can't you leave him alone, Charlie. He ain't done nothing."

Suzy steps up, as though she were drawn to the iron.

The pimp laughs. "Look at this, now he's hiding behind a dyke. Get out of the way, sawed-off hairless cunt."

Cunt. Hairless cunt. She lunges, not even thinking about the knife tucked in her boot, kicking instead for the balls. Feels the iron glance off her shoulder. Swings her fists, screaming her head off. Cunt hairless cunt hairless cunt hairless cunt... It's the screaming that puts him off more than the pummelling. Freezes him, freezes everyone in the street—the whores, the pimp, the passing students, Rudy. All frozen. By the immensity of her rage.

And even in full flight outside my body soaring in the pure white weightless sky of rage cunt she knows they are frozen cunt knows she has won and she can, had better, come down now or risk the worst cunt. I keep going anyway, just a moment longer, open-throated cunt soaring just a little higher, coasting on the sound of my own voice, the empty sky, the clear white waves of power flowing over her, through her, like some perfect drug cunt. Just a little longer, one more second. Okay all right that's it I'm done it's over I'm okay everything is fine I'm okay now we'll just go. Never mind. Forget it. Come on. Rudy. Come. On. We're. Going.

Crosstown Buses Run All Night
Doo da Doo da

All morning he's dragged his cross through the deserted canyon between the grey stone columns of the old-money banks and Anglo power on St. James Street—Canadian Imperial, Molson's, *The Gazette*—to Bleury, then west again on des Fortifications to Victoria Square. Here, de Maisonneuve must turn north and make his way downtown. Emerging from the narrow cobbled street, he is momentarily overcome by the scope and proportions of the triple-lane expressways, parking lots, glass towers that separate him from the city centre. Even the cross on his back, which seemed so monumental in the old city, has shrunk here, though it's lost none of its weight. And rising up before him like a curtain of water, another reason to pause: Beaver Hall Hill. Which he must now climb. Against the runoff and the rain and the elbowing secretaries and clerks running beneath umbrellas.

And the voices calling him. *Teiethinonhwera:ton ne Ietsi'nisten:ha tsí Iohontsa:te. Calling him to join his spirit to theirs in praise of the Earth our Mother.*

Even raising his head into the full force of the rain and shouting at the top of his darkened lungs, he can barely hear his own prayer: O Virgin of virgins, Mother of the world incarnate, help me now: give me the strength to climb this hill and the courage to resist pride should I succeed.

Kahnekaronnion. Spirit of water...

Bathe me, gentle Mary, in your merciful tears, flood my eyes with your pain that I may turn away from glory, bind my arms that I may not raise my hand against another, shut my mouth, choke the flow of empty words in my throat.

La rue de la Gauchetière. He swallows hard to forestall a coughing fit and takes the first step on the steep slope of Beaver Hall.

Spirit of water that quenches our thirst and purifies our lives.

Give me the determination to be unremarkable, to let the other man pass before me, to remain silent when I am bursting with answers, to suffer every trial without complaint, to go unnoticed, to fail at that at which I am best, to do my duty without reward, to die and be forgotten.

Hear us Great Spirit, we are the Rotinonhsion:ni, People of the Long House, People of the Great Splendour, People of the Great Peace, the Great Harmony, the Circle of Life.

He begins to move again. Almost immediately he realizes he will never make it up this street, and he has not even allowed himself to think about the climb up the mountain itself; because, assuming he can make it through the crowds downtown, there remains the Peel Street hill from Sherbrooke to Doctor Penfield, which is as bad as Beaver Hall, and then the muddy slope in the park and the two hundred and ten terrible steps to the lookout.

In spite of everything, he continues a little while longer, forcing one foot in front of the other, oblivious to the people who, in the rain coming down like broken glass, can't spare much more than a passing glance at this broken pilgrim and the scrapheap on his back. But in the doorway of the Hambourgeois–Chiens-chauds–Frites lunch bar which feeds the office buildings, his lungs finally grind him to a halt.

If France had given more support. If they had not given the governor-generalship to that thief de Lauzon and his sons. If the Jesuits… The Jesuits. Sometimes he dreams he is surrounded by Jesuits and not Iroquois; the arrows that pierce his chest are Jesuit arrows, the enemy wear long robes and carry twisted roods…

But no, he will not lapse into recriminations. He will think instead of Jeanne Mance. Her matter-of-fact way of dealing with adversity: refusing to give in to bitter feelings, yet refusing to give in. Jeanne Mance. Her steadfast devotion to the mission, her patience with the children and the sick, her clear-sightedness, her gentle eyes. No, not her eyes, he has forbidden himself to think of Jeanne that way. Instead he must concentrate on his prayer. Sweet Mother Mary, immaculate and chaste, sweet Virgin of Sorrows, serpent and moon at Your feet, my sins are daggers in Your heart.

Teiethinonhwera:ton ne Ietsi'sotha Ahsonthénkha Karáhkwa. We offer our greetings to our Grandmother the Moon.

Of course, there's only one thing to do: retreat, circumvent the obstacle, take the long way round, perhaps east through Chinatown and up Saint-Laurent...but that way there would still be the climb to Sherbrooke. Everywhere a steep hill stands between him and the final ascent. Unless. The underground route: walk west to the Place Bonaventure complex, go inside and down to subway level, along the winding subterranean passageway through the train station and over to Place Ville-Marie, emerging on Sainte-Catherine in the heart of downtown and at the foot of Mont-Royal. Of course he will have to watch out for the security guards in the station and the various shopping malls along the way, but he'll be out of the rain, and the string of escalators will ease his journey.

Getting the cruciform in the door to the Place Bonaventure is not easy, but once in out of the rain, he can lay it down in the long hallway and sit for a while to dry off under the mildly amused glances of passing strangers. Then it's through a maze of corridors and boutiques, down to the métro level and through the tunnel to the train station. As he steps into the vast open cathedral, a feeling of relief sweeps over him. Here, at last, the strange voices are gone. The station is filled with an all-embracing and supremely comforting silence: the hollow silence of churches, of minute sounds amplified — the click of a heel, a coin popping on a counter — the echoing silence of crowds in transit. He is suddenly overcome by a kind of pleasant weariness, so powerful he is prepared to lie down anywhere. Luckily there are plastic moulded seats available along the edge of the stairways leading down to the trains. He lays his cross against the barrier and eases himself into a chair, closing his eyes and abandoning himself to the muffled perfume of trains. Dozing. His mind as empty and cavernous as the great hall. His pilgrimage, his mission, forgotten. Then suddenly, a voice, unlike the others, booming, harsh, bilingual and barely decipherable: Votre attention s'il vous plaît: le train numé-mé-ro-ro-roo cinkrach-dieuuuuux, le York, en provenanchnack de Toron...trop, Guy...woof, Osheewawaaaaa, Kingshtong Écoerenwall entre en gâwwre à la foie numér-ro-ro-roo chaizzzzz; Your attention pleashhhh...te...rain numb...ber filthy-choo from Tirana, Guilt...would, Awchihuahua, Kinkstoned and Pornfall is now deriding on krack nubber sickshteeeeeee...eee...ee...

Recruitment Figures Up

Le Corbusier steps out of the elevator and onto the plush carpet of the outer office. Ah, this is more like it. Of course, there are no signs to indicate the identity of the establishment, but the carpet, the dark mahogany desk, the upholstered chairs — the scent of Rockefeller is everywhere. Except for the two pathetic figures camping on the long sofa and only partially screened by the potted kumquat: an unlikely duo of vagabonds, grey-maned professor and ragtag military deserter. Strangely, though by all appearances the two have been here a long time (the professor seems to be dozing), no one has put them out. But then the reception area seems to be unattended; perhaps the secretary has gone for help. Le Corbusier settles cautiously into the seat farthest from the intruders. As he does so, the military man, who may be wounded or at least having difficulty with his breathing, rises and, wincing imperceptibly, tries the door to the right. The door being clearly locked, the man turns to address Le Corbusier.

"If it's El Líder Maximo you've come for, he's not seeing anyone."

Le Corbusier smiles indulgently. "I'll just wait for the receptionist."

"Suit yourself." The man in fatigues shrugs and returns a wryer version of Le Corbusier's smile. "If he won't see us, I doubt he has time for you."

"I am expected," Le Corbusier announces.

"I was with him from the start, in Mexico. On the Granma."

"We have been corresponding," exclaims the architect, brandishing a handmade copy of his letter addressed to Mr. Rockefeller. "Now we are at the crossroads; the alliance between Le Corbusier and the captains of industry is within reach. This is a historic meeting, the dawn of a new age for all mankind: mass housing, health and prosperity for all…"

Ramón, having plucked the letter out of the other's gesturing hand and scanned the contents, tosses it back at the architect. "Rockefeller rules the globe…philosopher-king…magnificent artist. Pathetic trash!

The peoples of the world are rising up to take their destiny in hand and Le Corbusier grovels at the feet of monopoly capital, lyricizes imperialism, begs an audience with Caesar."

"Will your 'peoples of the world' build my skyscrapers?"

"When the people take power you'll find out. Do you think the Rocke-fellers of the world will build housing for the masses? First things first. You have been offered the opportunity to join the revolution; how many times has the Party invited you?"

Le Corbusier shrugs and turns to the Librarian. "Je leur ai dit qu'ils devaient se joindre à moi."

"Arrogance is the enemy of the revolution," barks Ramón.

"You confuse politics and art. Art is in its essence arrogant."

"It's just that kind of individualist, petit-bourgeois, opportunist talk that...that...Tania turning in the clearing by the radio, brown hair hanging loose down to her shoulders, blue-grey eyes...Aleida and the children wait-ing back in Cuba. Tania la Guerrillera...a trap? Was she, all along, an agent of the East Germans? KGB? Slipping in and out of the zone, carrying news, supplies, her husky voice. And always moving. Even her name shifting. Laura Gutiérrez Baur, Laura Gutiérrez de Martínez, Mary Aguilera, María Aguilera, Elma, Emma, Nadja, Haydee Tamara Bunke Bider. Simply 'T'. Was it weakness? A trap? Thrown together by the current of history. Her shoulder when she bent by the radio. And Aleida and the children, faithful, waiting silently in Cuba. Betrayal...weakness...the huskiness in her voice..." Ramón breaks off, wheezing and reaching for his old Ventolin pump.

"You would set fire to the cities, flood the streets in blood," Le Corbu-sier jumps in, ignoring the other's drifting discourse and taking advantage of his asthmatic fit, "when that all is needed is intelligent planning and imagination."

Guevara/Ché/Ramón, doubled over and wracked with coughing, refuses to yield. The Librarian has taken hold of his arm and is trying to pull him down beside him on the sofa, but he resists, waving his free arm at the Switzer and scraping a handful of air up from his lungs to respond: "You...think...substitute architecture for class struggle...cure the world...with a truckload of cement...won't happen...can't put an end to poverty...injustice with a mathematical formula." Ramón collapses into the Librarian's arms. *Tania, her blue-grey eyes in the clearing… Aleida, gentle, betrayed, bending over Camilio, their youngest… Hilda, his first wife abandoned… Quebrada del Yuro, the old woman standing in the canyon among her grazing goats, her dark eyes staring into his heart…*

"Mathematics," Le Corbusier sighs, and his eyes begin to glaze, "is the door to the absolute, the infinite, the prehensile and the unknowable. But there are walls which bar our way. Occasionally a door appears; a man opens it, enters, he is in another place: a land of gods, a land containing the secret keys to all the great systems. Door to miracles. Beyond this door, one no longer deals with men: one touches the universe. Before him shining combinations unfold without end like so many magic carpets. He stands there, enraptured in this radiant and magnificent light. He has entered the land of numbers."

"Better take an army along," croaks Ramón from his seat, "if you plan to get through that door."

"I require no armies; I have Modulor. A simple ribbon…let me show you," and Le Corbusier reaches into his pocket for the little canister. But the tape measure is not there. Gone. Vanished. Ramón and the old man watch as Charles-Édouard Jeanneret performs the gradual progression that characterizes all fruitless searches, from methodical patience through irritation and perspiration to panic. Suddenly he remembers. Stops, freezes, as he froze down in the shopping mall in the gaze of the Argosian Queen. Whispers her name.

Ramón smiles weakly. "That old woman picked your pocket?"

Le Corbusier is still in shock. "Modulor. She took the Modulor."

The old man nods his head, mumbles a few scorched syllables: "…my card…mé…tro…"

"She stole the Modulor," Le Corbusier repeats.

"A real pro, that one." Ramón shakes his head and rises to his feet. Already he is feeling better.

Le Corbusier turns on Ramón, seizing him by one crumpled lapel. "Where is she?"

"Long gone by now," Ramón replies, brushing away the dapper little man's hand and thumping one last fist on the closed office door. "Back up in the hills. Where we're going."

Dear Fidel

April 1, 1965

Fidel,

I hereby renounce formally my positions in the leadership of the party, my post as minister, my rank as comandante, my status as citizen.

At this moment I remember many things — when I met you in Maria Antonia's house in Mexico, when you suggested my coming, all the tensions involved in the preparations. I cannot deny that I am disappointed we could not meet once more. But it is all for the best. Other mountains of the world claim the aid of my modest efforts. I am able to do what is denied to you because of your responsibility, and the hour has come for us to part.

I shall carry to new battlefields the faith that you inculcated in me, the revolutionary spirit of my people, the feeling of fulfilling the most sacred of duties: to fight against imperialism wherever it is. This comforts and sufficiently cures any wound.

I am not sorry that I leave my children and my wife nothing material. I am happy it is so. I ask nothing for them, as I know the state will provide enough for their expenses and education.

I would like to say much to you and to our people, but I feel it is not necessary. Words cannot express what I would want them to, and I don't believe in bantering phrases.

In a revolution, one triumphs or one dies.

Ché

Let's Beat Up the Poor

Their progress is slowed not only by the rain and the old Librarian, whom Ché must practically carry, but by Le Corbusier's stubborn and occasionally acrobatic determination to keep the mud off his shoes. Plus there's the extra knapsack full of the old man's books which he refused to leave behind and which the architect refuses to carry. And then there's the dog. At least, though his pace is far from energetic, Pilote carries his own weight. But Ché has no fondness for dogs.

"Keep that Spaniard's lion cub away from me."

Le Corbusier shrugs. "This one's name is Pilote and he's French."

But Ché has already slipped into his favourite, Neruda: "Balboa, your dog was your soul: with his bloodstained jowls, picked up the slaves escaping, sank his Spanish teeth into the panting throats. A curse on dog and man...the horrible howl in the unbroken forest..."

And yet, in spite of the dog, the hard work and the quality of his recruits, Ché is relieved to be out of the llano—that white plain full of danger and temptation—and moving up into the cool Sierra. He can already feel the heady air of the Zona Roja.

They are in the park. Behind them, the circular tower of the Faculty of Medicine and the long hill they have climbed from the Peel Street subway. Ahead, an option. The dirt path winding its way gradually around and up le Mont-Royal, or the two hundred and ten wooden stairs straight up to the Mirador. Ché calls a rest stop and eases the Librarian down onto the grass under the trees. The old man offers an apologetic smile before plunging back into his book. Le Corbusier selects a rock and seats himself, but not before laying his cineral handkerchief down to protect his trousers. Guevara takes a shot of his Ventolin and opens his diary.

November 7, 1966. Ñancahuazú, southeastern Bolivia. In a canyon between the Serranías de las Pirirendas to the east and the Serranías Incahuasi to the west. Exuberant vegetation but scant water. So far no animals, but I expect to encounter big game: tigers and bears perhaps. Also plenty of deer, monkeys, iguanas, parrots, wild turkeys and the small black visna bird typical of this region.

He pauses, looks up, gazing to the south; somewhere in that direction the mountains join to form the Salta range at the foot of the Cordillera Oriental of the Andes. Argentina. Home. As close as he's come. To the dream. To carry the revolution home, one foco insurreccional at a time, a chess knight skipping across the continent, the circling steps of a minuet, back to the Andes and down to his beloved pampas.

A helicopter circles above them and back over the downtown traffic. Ché puts his journal away. No time to dream; he must bring his new recruits back to the camp. Slips his left arm under the Librarian's shoulder and slings his mochila over the other. Within a dozen steps, his asthma has begun to take hold and they have to halt again. He lights the last scrapings of dried clarín leaves in his pipe and manages to draw a couple of desperate puffs which bring no relief. They are about to begin climbing again when Pilote suddenly points and breaks into his characteristic coughing wheeze.

"Never mind that old mutt," Le Corbusier says. "He probably imagines he smells Iroquois."

Ché springs into action: he drags the Librarian under the railing and into the brush, and deploys Le Corbusier and himself in ambush at the foot of the stairs. The dog, meanwhile, has made himself comfortable and quiet in the wet grass, although his eyes remain open. For several minutes there is no sign of movement. Then the laborious breathing of climbers and, soon after, peering through the bushes, Ché can make out two figures climbing toward them.

Alegría de Pío. His baptism of fire. Pinned down by enemy fire on all sides, forced to retreat, he chose to save the box of ammunition instead of the medical kit. This time there is no ammunition box; only a knapsack of books. And the enemy is advancing, oblivious to their trap. A few more steps. Now. He is in mid-leap over the railing and shouting for Le Corbusier to do the same when he recognizes Suzy Creamcheez and has to twist and roll to avoid the sharp point of the blade she has already whipped into action. He lands in a heap at the feet of her bizarre gaucho companion, who screams in terror and steps behind her.

"Jesus, it's Ché," Suzy says, slipping the knife back into her boot. "I thought you were a mugger."

Ché picks himself up slowly. "Don't use that name here. I am called Fernando."

Suzy shrugs. "Fernando, Tatu, Mongo, Ramón…whatever… I can't keep track." She steps aside. "This here is Rudy, my hero."

"Rodolpho Alfonzo Rafaelo Pierre Filibert Guglielmi di Valentino d'Antonguolla," Rudy amends.

Ché eyes the elaborate gaucho outfit doubtfully. "Is he Peronista?"

"What does he mean?" Rudy asks, his hand straying to the top button of his shirt. "If he's insulting my manhood…"

"Where's the old woman?" A voice in the bushes: Le Corbusier, only now emerging to dust himself off and confront Suzy. "That Greek stole my Modulor."

Suzy ignores him and starts up the steps. The three men follow. One. Two. Three. Four. Five. Six. Seven. Eight. Nine. Ten. Eleven. Twelve… suddenly Ché remembers the old Librarian. Eleven. Ten. Nine, eight, sevensixfivefourthreetwoone. They find him where they left him, deeply immersed in the bushes and Dr. Henry Julian Hunter's *Report on the Excessive Mortality of Infants in Some Rural Districts of England, 1861.*

"Because if there is anyone," Rudy says, watching Ché help the old man onto the stairs, "anyone who doubts my manhood, I challenge that person to a personal contest…"

"Come on, give us a hand," Ché says, and passes the Librarian over to Suzy, who grudgingly takes his weight on her shoulder. Ché picks up the bag of books and they attack the steps a second time.

Rudy leaps ahead and displays his right biceps. "A duel would be illegal. But in America, boxing is legal; so is wrestling." Ché brushes past. "I therefore defy anyone to meet me in the boxing or wrestling arena to prove in the American way which of us is the real man."

Eight. Nine. Ten. "That old woman better be up there," Le Corbusier grumbles, falling in behind.

"Because I am an American citizen," Valentino says, addressing himself to Pilote, now that the others have all filed past. "I possessed three Cadillacs."

The hound manifests no interest, blinks once, eyes the back of the mounting column for a moment, shakes the water off his ears and, instead of following, lowers his haunches to the ground.

Eleven. Twelve. Thirteen. Fourteen. "Is that dog purebred?" Valentino asks. He has always liked dogs. Well, collected them anyway. Along with the cars, the cameras, the armour, and the Arabian horses. But the dogs were his favourites. Natasha and her mob of Pekinese. The Doberman that monsieur Hebertot of the Théâtre des Champs-Élysées gave him on their last day in Paris. "If this animal is pure, I will buy him. Name your price."

Le Corbusier glances back at the seated dog. "Pilote! What's the matter with you?"

Ché halts. Surveys the surrounding bushes. Bends close to the stairs to listen for footsteps. Nothing. He straightens and sighs. "Maybe he smells something. There is some evidence the Mayans could have come this far north..."

"Pilote," Le Corbusier calls.

The dog sits, impassive.

"It's the stairs," Suzy ventures.

"We'll have to leave him," says Ché.

Le Corbusier hesitates. "I can't," he says, "cette bête est le chien du sieur de Maisonneuve."

Thirteentwelveeleventen...

Suzy leans the Librarian against the railing and massages her shoulder. "I don't like this dog."

"He was placed in my care."

Ché puffs on his empty pump and glares at the tricked-up architect. "Someone...will have to...carry him."

Le Corbusier eyes the muddy dog and the line of drool dangling from its jowls. "I can take the books," he offers.

Valentino gazes into the trees.

"We'll have to take the path," says Ché, pocketing the Ventolin. "It's a long walk, winding round all the way instead of straight up..."

"It sure beats these stairs," Suzy insists, "unless one of you tough guys wants to give me a hand with the old man."

Pilote lifts a leg to mark the bottom step before starting up the path.

The Average Hero

"To take possession of space is the first act of living beings, men and beasts, plants and clouds, those fundamental manifestations of equilibrium and existence in time." Le Corbusier, slightly dusty and hoarse from the long trek up the mountain, haranguing his new audience.

"Great," Suzy complains, "that's all we need around here: another visionary with a compulsive personality disorder and a tendency to flights of ideas."

"He's only angry because we took the winding path," says Ché.

"Are we donkeys?" Le Corbusier wants to know. "Man walks in a straight line because he has a goal; he knows where he is going; he has made up his mind to reach some particular place and he goes straight to it."

"Not that he would have picked up the damned dog himself," Ché mutters as he makes certain the Librarian is comfortable in his bunk.

"Winding roads," Le Corbusier continues, "lead to cities sinking to nothing, to chaos, anarchy, the overthrow of ruling classes."

"A woman gets there any way she can," says Lady Macbeth on her knees, working to get the fire started.

Clytæmnestra twists in her bunk, searching for a position to relieve her aching back. "I've given him his filthy ribbon; why can't he leave us in peace?"

Le Corbusier hesitates, fingering his recovered treasure, then returns to the central theme of his presentation. Because street planning was, in point of fact, as he now willingly acknowledges (he is in a fine mood since the witch returned the ribbon), a minor digression from his principal topic. "Modulor is anthropocentric; it is the measure of man. And more: le Modulor has cracked open a door, a door through which we glimpse the miracle of numbers."

"I beg you," Ché barks, having now moved over to check on Rudy, who has begun to tinker with the radio, "we've already heard the ode to mathematics. English feet, French metres, Persian zars, Greek pecheus: we don't need another measurement."

"That is my point, exactly," Le Corbusier shouts, whipping his ribbon in Ché's direction. "Modulor puts an end to the chaos of competing standards."

Suzy launches into a Modulorian mantra: "One metre thirteen to two metres twenty-six, one metre eighty-three to three metres sixty-six, two metres ninety-six to five metres ninety-two…"

"Power," the guerrilla leader wheezes, "determines the standards of measurement. In Japan, the Kyoto or peasant ken, as you should know, measured one metre ninety-seven, fifteen centimetres more than the Tokyo version. Well, once the emperors took up residence in Tokyo, that was the end of the Kyoto ken…"

"Is Modulor merely *a* universal measurement, or is it *the* universal measurement?"

"…four metres seventy-nine to nine metres fifty-seven…"

"Are there countless paths leading to the miracle? Or have I, Le Corbusier, discovered the one, the only door? To answer this question, we must undertake a voyage."

"Here's the door," grumbles Clytæmnestra. "Don't forget your bags."

But the architect is warming to his subject. "We stand, ladies and gentlemen, before the Cistercian ruins at the Abbaye de Chaalis in Ermononville. Admire the magnificent doorway, the harmony of its proportions. Dating back to the thirteenth century!" Fumbling in his bag, Le Corbusier produces a postcard of said ruins, which he passes around before returning to his precious ribbon. "Now let us measure the height and width. Et voilà! Two hundred twenty-six on the Modulor scale. I measure the depth: three hundred sixty-six! I am happy. Now, at last, the width of the door: one hundred thirteen! Moral of the story: they knew the secret of the Modulor. On employait la section d'or!"

"One metre thirteen to two metres twenty-six, one metre eighty-three to three metres sixty-six…"

"On to the temple of Séti the First in Abydos. Think of the Egyptians: their art, their imperial elegance, la rigueur, l'implacable fermeté. Measure the temple! A perfect set of proportions identical to those of the Modulor.

Now locate the very centre of the temple. You will find there, at the heart of a hieroglyphic inscription, a minuscule disc which has attracted the eye of Le Corbusier, trained as it is to the tracing of lines. And what is this figure inscribed in the centre of the tiny disc? C'est le Modulor!"

"…two metres ninety-six to five metres ninety-two…"

"Notre-Dame de Paris: exquisite cathedral at the heart of the city of light. Measure it! Modulor!" Le Corbusier pauses long enough to provide another visual aid: a black grid of Modulorian lines superimposed on a photograph of Notre-Dame de Paris. "This ribbon has never left my pocket since"—he casts a dark glance at Clytæmnestra—"well, almost never. I carry it everywhere. All that is beautiful, the great classics, Man's achievements throughout the ages: all are based on Modulor!"

And now on to the practical segment of his presentation. "I am going to show you how Le Corbusier arrived at his discovery. Take a man, an average man."

Suzy comes forward, volunteering, but, as she is clearly neither man nor average, Corbu impatiently rejects her and selects himself instead as a model. He raises his right arm, holding the end of the Modulor tape above his head. "An average man, approximately one metre seventy-five, his hand raised. This is l'homme le bras levé. Now place him in two squares of one metre ten." He runs quickly through the calculations and concludes: "Employing this grid, based on a man placed within, you will arrive at a series of measurements, a logarithmic series of proportions, which perfectly marry human stature and the science of mathematics."

"Yes," says Suzy, advancing with sudden interest and her own arm held high, "but Corbu honey, are you saying this Modulor thing, this universal measurement, the whole thing starts with the height of an average man?"

"Yes, yes, of course. That is the foundation: one metre seventy-five."

Ché, standing several centimetres above the architect's standard, laughs: "I think he means the average Frenchman."

"As a rule," Lady Macbeth interjects, "the French are a short people."

"The African Zulu," Clytæmnestra yawns, "measures something over two metres."

"Come here, Rudy," Suzy calls to the Italian gaucho, who is still sulking over his Cadillac adventure. "Let's measure Rudy; I mean, shit, ain't he the

King of Romance, the Prince of Sex Appeal, the Screen's Greatest Lover, the Sheik of Araby? Let's see if your Modulor measures up to Rudy."

"I am speaking of the norm; not some larger-than-life fiction," Le Corbusier objects, looking around at the assembled company for support and wishing de Maisonneuve were here.

"Surely," says Ché, "you don't intend to base this universal measurement on less than exemplary men? I calculate the new socialist man will measure six feet, at least."

"A hallucinatory premise. Where's your data?"

Suzy is already rifling through the Librarian's bag of books. "You want data?"

As he stepped from the sleek scarlet sports car and came toward her, she had barely time to take in the dark well-groomed hair, the leather flying jacket sitting comfortably on broad shoulders, the long legs encased in thigh-hugging jeans, the loping strides, before he was directly in front of her. She felt the firm grip of his hands on her waist and saw the straight line of a jaw that spoke of power beyond physical strength, the confidence of a man in control, the kind of man she had always dreamed of. When finally she allowed herself to look into his eyes, she felt her whole body sinking into the calm, dark gaze. Her heart beat wildly. He moved closer and, in that instant, even before he kissed her, she knew this man smiling down on her from his height of six feet was the man of her dreams...

She got up slowly and swayed toward me with enough sex appeal to stampede a businessman's lunch. "You're cute," she said. "I'm cute, too." Her smile was tentative, but could be persuaded to be nice. I slapped her around a little. She didn't mind the slaps. I set to work on the dress. She didn't mind that, either. She let me hold her arms up and she spread her fingers out wide, as if that was cute. She fell into my arms giggling. "You're just a big tease." Then she turned her body slowly and lithely. She tilted herself toward me on her toes and fell straight back into my arms. I caught her under her arms and she went rubber-legged on me instantly. I had to hold her close to hold her up. When her head was against my chest she screwed it around and asked, "Who are you?"

"Marlowe," I said. "I'm a dick."

She giggled. "I like my men tall," she said. "How tall are you?"

"Six feet," I told her.

"That would be one point eighty-three metres," she calculated. "You're a big dick."

The Marshal had seen the rider coming from a long ways off, loping through the mesa scrub with the sun at his back. Almost immediately he knew it was the Kid, just from the way he rode, and from the size and speed of the mare beneath him.

"Brown Bitch," the Marshal muttered under his breath and spat into the dust. Brown Bitch was the Kid's horse and folks who knew had told him that the Brown Bitch was just about the only living thing the Kid had ever cared anything about.

For a long time the Marshal stood in the doorway and watched man and horse coming, as though he hoped they might change direction or he'd been mistaken and it wasn't the Kid after all but some lone buffalo hunter heading across the plain. But the mare kept coming hard and straight. Finally she dipped out of sight into a dry gully and the Marshal turned back into the room, unlocked the rack and took the Winchester and strapped on his Colt. When he got back to the door the Kid was already within rifle range, a clear target, all six feet of him standing straight up in the saddle, hatless and grinning wildly.

FULL SHOT — *The desert*

    A vast sandy waste. Silhouetted on the crest of a dune, the Sheik astride his Arabian steed.

CLOSE SHOT

    The Sheik riding hard through the desert.

FULL SHOT — *The oasis*

    An encampment in the oasis, including the main tent.

INTERIOR — *Inside the tent*

    Among the carpets and cushions and hookahs, the lovely English girl paces, full of apprehension.

EXTERIOR — *Outside the tent*

    The Sheik rides into the encampment and swiftly dismounts.

WIDE SHOT, INTERIOR — *Inside the tent*

> *The Sheik strides into the tent. The English maiden retreats to the far corner of the tent, trembling in fear. The Sheik surveys his prize, relishing her beauty. He advances toward her, scornful of her protestations, cuts off her escape, seizes her upheld wrists, pulls her to him, takes her in his strong arms, presses her trembling body to him. She struggles, but to no avail. He smiles, enjoying the contest, pauses to fix her in his mesmerizing gaze. Towers over her from his six-foot height. Then the kiss: violent at first, as she struggles against him, beating at his shoulders with her hand; then, as she gradually succumbs, deeper and deeper and finally tender.*

"The worst part is that, from Rockefeller's point of view, and Rockefeller is the guy you're trying to sell the idea to," Suzy suggests, "the average man is an American."

Le Corbusier is aghast. "Mon dieu, she's right! Rockefeller will be thinking of Americans. Merde. How tall is the average American hero?"

"Malcolm X stood well over six feet," offers Ché, "before they shot him."

"Ce n'est pas grave," says Le Corbusier, already unrolling his sheets of drawings on the ground and searching through his things for ruler and compass. "A minor adjustment. Of course, I should have known. En fait, la taille du héro est de six pieds. The Modulor must grow. L'homme, de six pieds, donc, le bras levé. Now place him in two squares of one metre ten. Fais jouer à cheval sur les deux carrés, un troisième carré qui fournit la solution. Le lieu, de l'angle droit, pour situer ce troisième carré…"

"Ladies and gentlemen," announces Clytæmnestra, "the great Le Corbusier adjusts the universal measurement."

"Basketball players, I am told," says Rudy, leaning over Le Corbusier's shoulder, "are currently very popular in America."

"When the pure forms collapsed," Ché cites Lorca, "in the cri-cri of the daisies, it came to me that they had murdered me."

Le Corbusier freezes, drops compass, pencil, ruler and much of his enthusiasm onto the spread of papers at his feet. "These references, these books," he says, leafing through a paperback, "they can be consulted?" He moves to the edge of the camp to gaze down at the university campus at the foot of the mountain. "I admit," he announces, having already regained some of his energy, "more extensive research is required," and he turns back to his audience: "Who has a library card?"

Mustard Seeds, Shards of Glass

Anger?

His own ragged image in the glass wall of the Cathcart Street exit of the Place Ville-Marie shopping promenade. Though, standing inside the exit, he can see la rue Sainte-Catherine a block north and the crest of Mont-Royal, his destination, dominating the city, there is no way to fit his crucifix through the revolving doors.

Under the circumstances, anger would have been perfectly justified. In fact, it was expected. He could see it in the eyes of everyone in the mission, once the word was out—even Jeanne Mance, for all her piety—all of them anticipating anger, and probably they would have welcomed it. At least some attempt to contact Paris, or the Saint-Sulpice Seminary. Because, technically, the seminary was the sole body with the authority to relieve him of his duties. A technicality the nature of which Lieutenant-General de Tracy understood full well. Which is why he had formulated the order as a permission: "Permission to return to France, to attend to your personal business." But de Maisonneuve had not requested permission to return to France. He had no personal affairs which required attention. And then the added insult of naming Zacharie Dupuis to take command in his absence, "for as long as we shall deem necessary." In the past, whenever he had absented himself, it had been the Governor's privilege to name his replacement. The truth was he had been summarily stripped of his position. Without investigation, without the opportunity to explain himself. De Tracy's message was clear: Get out of New France. Go home. Find some hovel in Paris to live out your days.

Anger then. But he had felt no anger. He had contacted no one; neither the seminary nor Paris, nor anyone else. So not anger, but what then? Relief? Because the irony of the situation was that de Tracy's fears were, in point of fact, without any real foundation. The mission was a failure. De Maisonneuve represented no threat and, by then, barely an inconvenience. What had he achieved by banning the fur trade from Montréal, by refusing to award himself a concession or to enrich himself in some other way? By strictly adhering to his mission? Conversion of the savages? Not one had embraced God and the Church. Instead they had waged war against him. Wrapped the encampment in a siege of howling shadows, night terror, ambushed and slaughtered his men, set fire to the crops in the fields. The cross atop Mont-Royal. And the face of the man he had killed outside the gates of the fort.

And yet, the beginning had held such promise. May 8, 1642, early morning. The prairie speckled with flowers, birds of every colour and plumage. With Montmagny, le Père Vimont and a handful of faithful, he had landed at Place Royale. He had thrown himself on his knees. They had sung *Veni Creator*. Jeanne Mance and the other women prepared an altar. Madame de la Peltrie contributed her jewels. Le Père Vimont said mass. "Ce que vous voyez ici n'est qu'un grain de moutarde..." but sown by hands so pious, so full of the spirit of the faith... "que sans doute il faut que le Ciel ait de grands desseins...je ne fais aucun doute que ce petit grain ne produise un grand arbre." One day, Vimont had promised, that seed would make wonders, would multiply and cover the earth.

Meanwhile de Tracy and his kind, working out of Stadacona, had pushed their fur trade upriver, turning the countryside into a site of plunder, politics and murder. De Maisonneuve's mission a failure, those who had entrusted it to him all dead. Le Royer, who, standing before the great altar in Notre-Dame de Paris in 1635, had first received the vision to found a colony in Montréal. Le Père Lalemant, who had received a young soldier—twenty-five years old, Paul de Chomedey, a veteran of the Thirty Years War against the Dutch, devoted to the army but unable to bear the drunkenness and license of his fellow soldiers, and wanting to exercise his profession in a more edifying context, in New France perhaps, which he'd read about in a Jesuit *Relation* picked up in the offices of a friend's lawyer—Father Lalemant, who had received that young man and introduced him to Le Royer and the members of the Society of Notre-Dame to Convert the Savages, introduced him to his mission and his life. Le Royer, Lalemant, most of the members of the Society: all dead. And thank God for that; they would be spared the devastation of his failure.

What result then? No converts, no peace and devotion to the Mother of God in all Her magnificent purity. No mission. Only his own poverty. Because he was, after twenty-four years of sacrifice and hard labour, penniless. Only the six thousand pounds the mission store owed him, and his precious lute. He would leave both to the poor sheltering in Hôtel Dieu.

And the revolving glass doors too tight to pull the cross through. What to do then? Turn back? Drag his burden through the mall, down the escalator into the train station again? And then what? There would still be the hill to climb. The slashing rain. His aching shoulder. Seek out another exit? Risk capture, the patrolling security guards, confiscation of his treasure. Failure. Again. The Iroquois everywhere. Or dismantle the crucifix back into tin pipe, blown tire, leafy branches, glass shards, rusted street sign, and take it through the doors piece by piece? Blasphemy.

What then? Abandon his pilgrimage? But he'd nailed his promise on a parchment to the cross at the flood's edge. A pledge to God and the Virgin Mother. He would carry this rood to the summit of the mountain. And he can see the way ahead so clearly: the short walk across Sainte-Catherine, north to Sherbrooke and the gates of the university, across the gently sloping campus lawn, to the final steep climb through the thorny forest. Where are his voices now? Only silence. Only this transparent wall standing between him and his mission.

So: relief, then. Was that it? Or cowardice? To escape, to flee when it was already clear to anyone who was not completely blinded by faith that the mission was a failure — to flee before the long descent, the slide into becoming just another colony trading infested blankets, baubles and bad alcohol for the flesh of living animals. Greed, self-aggrandizement, corrupt government, fornication and commerce. The daily grind. To vanish from the site of his humiliation. To escape the trusting gaze of Marguerite Bourgeois and Jeanne Mance, his devoted allies, his followers, his failure. Once more across the ocean, but this time shut up alone in his cabin with neither food nor fresh air. To live out his days pinching pennies in a forgotten corner of Paris.

What then? Dismantle his cross? Abandon his mission? Turn back from this wall of glass? Drag his burden back through the mall? Down to the harbour? Across the sea in a cabin without air or food? What result? What was it? Anger? Cowardice? Relief?

He's dizzy. The earth trembles beneath his feet. The street, the mountain in the glass before him, shimmer and blur. He shakes his head, blinks. The shaking stops. Must be the weight of all these questions on his back. He takes a deep breath. But the tremor resumes, and with more force. He rests the tail of his cross on the ground behind him, fights to keep his balance, squinting to steady the scene beyond the doors, drawing long breaths to steady his heart. But it is not he that is shaking; it's the world around him. The ground. The street. The revolving doors. The wall of glass, rippling and then, suddenly, exploding, shattering into a million glass nails and falling like a curtain of rain to open the way before him.

Is This a Dagger?

L ate afternoon in a camp lethargic with hunger. Suzy lying open-eyed in her bunk, too weak to move, too famished to sleep. Lady Macbeth hunched over her small fire of twigs and scraps, barely murmuring above the simmering surface of her pot. Hunger has driven Le Corbusier to put aside his pencils and diagrams. Even Ché is content to sip his watery yerba maté, with the occasional unhappy glance at Rudy, whose tinkering has finally reduced the radio to pieces. The new recruits have brought nothing but books, more speeches and more mouths to feed. As for Pilote the dog, he has had the good sense to move off some ways into the brush, out of sight and off the list of options.

Such is the state of the camp when Clytæmnestra comes striding in from the forest, dangling a bloodied squirrel captured in one of the traps she has fabricated from the strands of her net and concealed in the under-brush here and there along the trail. Immediately, Suzy sits up in her bunk. In silence Clytæmnestra marches through the mud to the fire's edge and drops her prize by Lady Macbeth's lap. "Here, woman," she says, bending over to dip her bloody hands in the pot's not-quite-bubbling water. "Let's see if you can clean and cook that into something edible."

"Clean it yourself," Lady Macbeth growls, glancing quickly at the squirrel but making no move to take it.

"I'll clean it," Suzy says, dropping from her hammock.

Lady Macbeth raises a hand to stop the younger woman. "Is the great Queen Clytæmnestra too proud to sully her hands with woman's work?"

"Each of us does what she's best suited for," Clytæmnestra says, settling into her bunk without bothering to turn around. Then, turning on her elbow, in a single motion she pulls a dagger from the folds of her robe and flicks it into the ground inches in front of Lady Macbeth. "Here's something you've seen before, old woman. See if you can make proper use of it for once."

Suddenly and with surprising agility, Lady Macbeth is on her feet, knife in hand, but before she can move on Clytæmnestra's reclining figure, Suzy steps between them. "I don't mind," she says, gently prying the weapon from Lady Macbeth's fingers and carrying it back to the fire. Clytæmnestra, for her part, has settled back and closed her eyes without so much as a flinch.

Lady Macbeth glares at the reclining figure, then follows Suzy and reclaims the knife. "Fetch some wood for the fire," she mutters, staring for an instant at the blade. With a single practised stroke she slits the creature from head to tail and separates it from its skin. "Just as I thought: all bone and no meat," she grumbles. Then shouts after the departing Suzy: "Fetch me some toadstools and liverwort, and see if you can find a handful of nettles or cocksfoot."

"Nettles and cocksfoot," they can hear Suzy chanting as she disappears up the path.

"And for God's sake, don't bring me any of that damned stinkweed."

"Fetch her some bats and lizards and worms; the old witch will know what to do with them," Clytæmnestra scoffs from her bunk.

"I would, too," Lady Macbeth whispers, carving fingers of meat and dropping them into the pot. "I'd make a charm of powerful trouble."

"Fillet of snake, eye of newt and toe of frog," Clytæmnestra sings up into the branches.

"Can't you women be silent?" A shout from the area of what used to be the radio, where Rudy is rapidly approaching the limits of both his patience and his electronics skills.

"Nothing," says Le Corbusier, "is less attractive than a pair of peckish women."

Clytæmnestra sits up, angry. "I'll do some pecking soon."

"You'd best beware," Lady Macbeth calls out to Le Corbusier. "That's a man-killer speaking."

"And proud to say so," Clytæmnestra barks back. "As though that one were innocent of crime. See the blood on her hands?"

Lady Macbeth, crouching over the pot, stops to stare at her fingers, darkened with squirrel's blood. "Innocence has nothing to do with it," she says, muttering almost inaudibly as she launches into her compulsive hand-wringing. "Only a fool would wield the blade herself and seize the crown. Any woman knows enough to place a man before her as a shield."

"Any coward," Clytæmnestra fires back.

"A woman's power should be clothed in the robes of submission."

"Plotting and scheming like some tavern slut."

"I never murdered my own husband."

"You lacked the courage."

Finally the quarrelling rekindles Ché's speechifying: "The correct handling of contradictions among the people," he begins, rising from his post, "requires first that we distinguish contradictions among the people from contradictions with the enemy…"

"Shut up!" both women shout in unison. Ché retreats and the camp relapses into silence until Suzy steps back into the clearing, carrying branches and bits of inflammable debris she has gathered in the park. She lays her load down by the fire, pulls a clump of moss and mushrooms from inside her T-shirt and hands it to Lady Macbeth.

"I will admit," the old woman says, addressing the girl as though she had been present throughout the debate, "I am no Clytæmnestra, to kill a man and rule alone. I stood behind and pushed one forward. Plotted, yes. I schemed. I do not deny it. But I never shed my woman's robes for a man's trousers."

Clytæmnestra laughs. "With limbs like hers, t'were best she kept her skirts on."

But Lady Macbeth is too wrapped in her twisting, turning hands to take the bait. "I went too far. I should have kept to my woman's chamber and let events unfold. And I would have, had my Lord Macbeth, in his haste, not forgotten our plan and brought the bloody dagger back with him from the king's chamber."

"You put the dagger back," Suzy says.

"Some women," says Clytæmnestra, "are forever cleaning up after a man."

But Lady Macbeth is up and pacing, her hands winding and unwinding. "I called on the spirits: unsex me, thicken my blood, stop up the passage to remorse, turn my milk to green gall."

"Better to stand and fight," Clytæmnestra says, sitting up in her bunk, and Suzy, smiling, echoes, "Stand and fight!"

"Shout the truth," they continue in unison, "and let them do their worst."

"Keep it down," Rudy barks from the radio set. "What kind of women are these, shouting and flinging daggers? A truly beautiful woman is calm, serene. Her strength lies deeper."

Ché scoffs. "Spare me your celluloid women. Give me Baudelaire's woman: 'A heart abyssal in its depth, a soul confirmed in crime. Lady Macbeth, Æschylus's dream.'"

"There was a moment," Clytæmnestra says, lying back and her voice dropping to a dark whisper, "brief and too long ago to remember. A dozen years, a woman ruled in Argos. A dozen years to undo a murdering millennium. And even then, such a fragile throne, each day standing upon the ramparts, watching and waiting for the return of a son, of murder and the rule of men."

An eddying silence follows in the wake of Clytæmnestra's remembering. Finally Lady Macbeth clears her throat over the fire: "Notice there's no mention of the boyfriend. Has the adulteress forgotten a certain Ægisthus, then?"

Clytæmnestra shrugs. "Another coward," and sighs "—but a proficient lover."

Now the stew is cooked and the old debate, unresolved, peters out over the bubbling hell-broth.

"Ah," says Le Corbusier, coming over to examine Lady Macbeth's mixture, "Potage Créçy." He dips an empty soup can into the pot and, settling down by the fire to eat, completes his table d'hôte: "Paupiettes de sole Dugléré à la duxelle, fricadelles de veau Smitane à la béchamel, pommes à la Sarladaise and, for dessert, pêches Ninon, or no, rather Bombe Marinette."

Clytæmnestra does not deign to leave her bunk, but Suzy brings two busted aluminum pie plates to the fire.

Lady Macbeth ladles a portion onto each plate. "Heaven forbid her Highness should come and fetch her own food."

Clytæmnestra wipes her knife in preparation for her supper. "You'll all be eating leaves soon."

This is true. Soon, as the weather warms and city folk invade the park, even the squirrels will be too bloated with picnic scraps to bother going after Clytæmnestra's meagre bait.

"There'll be small game," Ché suggests, scarfing down the food with the energy and manners that earned him the nickname of El Chancho among the rebeldes of the Granma expedition. "Rabbits. And plenty of berries."

"Right," adds Suzy, "half-eaten hamburgers, rotting apple cores, gnawed-over chicken bones, the crumbs at the bottom of chip sacks."

Lady Macbeth leans over and taps Suzy on the tattoo. "You could make a decent marriage...with a bit of work."

"Please," Suzy brushes away the old woman's hand. "I'm eating."

Now, at last, Pilote lifts himself up and approaches cautiously to sniff the stew.

"Keep that hound away from me," Ché warns, "or so help me, I'll put him in the pot."

Tango Agamemnon

A campfire will suck all the light out of the night sky. Outside the band's small circle, a dog-hungry darkness prowls. The food has all been eaten. Le Corbusier is gone, set out for the library; Valentino is back at work on the radio. Only Suzy continues to gnaw on a scrap of rodent's bone, the last of their feast, while Ché hums an old Gardel favourite. "Caminito que el tiempo ha borrado, que juntos un día nos viste pasar..." Lady Macbeth picks up the tango on her mouth harp while Clytæmnestra shifts her position slightly to eye the hammock where they have laid the Librarian, exhausted from the trek up the mountain.

Who is this old man groaning and tossing in a kind of half sleep? Great grey head lolling to one side, tangled filthy mane spotted with tiny white balls of spittle. That face, somehow familiar. An old lover? An enemy? Remains of the iron-hearted warrior. Last of the Titans. She approaches, bends closer, trying to make out the restless muttering, the barely decipherable snippets of some ancient text.

"...a fetter...the monopoly...a fetter...the mode of production... sprung up...flourished along with...under..."

"...he venido por última vez," Ché hums, "he venido a contarte mi mal."

The fuliginous curls, the great white beard—a God visiting his subjects? Zeus on tour, come down with a fistful of lightning and a mouthful of wind, except that it would be difficult to imagine this wreck of a creature vanquishing Cronos, binding and gagging the father of all fathers, putting him away for a thousand eternities. No, not a God. Still, that face... Perhaps merely an old revolutionary who once long ago enlisted her in his great mission. A father preaching patience, hard work, sacrifice for the greater cause. Meanwhile she and her sisters waiting for their turn to come.

"...centralization...production...means..."

"...Caminito que entonces estabas bordeado de trébol y juncos en flor..."

Maybe not a God, after all. Ægisthus, son of Thyestes: lover, temporary ally, arms laden with promises, heart thirsting for vengeance against Agamemnon and the House of Atrides. Philosopher in women's robes. She recalls a certain fondness for Ægisthus. Didn't they sleep and plot together, rule the city, parry the old men's schemes, prepare the trap? Yet, in so many ways, Ægisthus was a disappointment. A short sexual attention span and, in the end, he let her do the hard killing.

"...the means...the end..."

No, not Zeus and not Ægisthus. Her husband then, returned once more, to replay their drama for the millionth time. Agamemnon cutting in for one last dance. A taste of the net, the thrust of her blade.

"That's what I can't understand," says Suzy, watching Clytæmnestra watching the Librarian. "I mean, what did you see in him?"

"...una sombra ya pronto serás..."

Lady Macbeth downs her harmonica and peers through the smoke of the fire at the figure in the hammock. "You're too young," she tells Suzy. "You never saw him in his prime. Bloody, bold, resolute. Laughing to scorn the power of men." She pauses, silent for a moment, then speaks to the fire: "For none of woman born shall harm Macbeth." Then looking back at Suzy. "So strong, so full of power."

"...una sombra, lo mismo que yo..."

"And handsome," adds Clytæmnestra.

Suzy steps closer to the bed and the crippled figure, shakes her head: "Right now, old Strong and Handsome smells pretty bad."

Lady Macbeth sighs and begins the slow washing motion of her hands. *There in the darkness above the flames, an image clear and sharp. A child, yellow curls in a jewelled crown. Ah, Macbeth, you failed me at the fateful hour. Stood whimpering and trembling before a king.* Shaking off the memory with a shiver, she turns back to Suzy: "You're too young; you can't remember."

"I was old enough this afternoon. Carried his useless carcass over a mile of stinking mud. And uphill all the way... Not that he weighs much."

"A hundred years ago," Clytæmnestra recalls, "we were young; he stood tall, straight, unflinching. And a voice like music: David's harp, a chorus of angels. Words flowing in a river of crystals. He showed us a city without walls, green promenades, honeyed fountains... Golden days, golden promises."

Suzy shrugs. "What they won't say to get their pus-filled dicks inside your shorts."

"…una sombra, lo mismo que yo."

Clytæmnestra bends over the reclining figure.

Great King Agamemnon, ruler of Argos, conqueror of Troy. My husband. When I wed you, I wed a serpent. Promised Greeks a century of peace and justice. Promised to be father to my children; not a sun would slip beneath the earth that you would not lie beside me in our bed.

"There," says Suzy, "what did I tell you?"

Clytæmnestra, standing now and turning slowly on her heel.

Nights on end we lay together. Your hand on my thigh. The small of my back. Caressed me. Never tiring. Your tongue on my breast. Inside me.

A groan from Suzy.

Lady Macbeth circles the fire to kiss Suzy lightly on the cheek. "Don't worry. That doesn't last long. After the first flush of victory, they can barely stay awake long enough to tinkle in the sheet."

Clytæmnestra spinning at the edge of darkness. You promised peace and gave us war. And a widow's vengeful spite, as well. Lay with me at night and in the morning slew my daughter. Your flocks were rich and teeming in their fleece, but you sacrificed your child instead. Murdered the agony I laboured into love to charm away the savage winds of Thrace.

"Leave him alone," says Ché, interrupting his song.

"Leave her alone," Suzy barks with a quick glare of warning in Ché's direction while she wraps her arms round Clytæmnestra to break the spinning spell.

Suddenly the old Librarian opens his eyes, trying to sit up, shouts: "The integument is burst asunder!"

"Now, you've woken him," Ché complains.

"Never mind," Lady Macbeth says to the old man, bending over to tuck him in again. "You've had another dream."

"The knell of private property!" cries the Librarian.

"Ding, dong," sings Suzy. "Tinkle, tinkle."

"Wake up, old man," Clytæmnestra shouts from Suzy's arms. "Where are your armies of ardent followers now?"

"Gone off and left him with the women," says Suzy.

"Followers?" Valentino scoffs, looking up from the pile of rubble that used to be the radio. "Look where all those ardent followers have got him."

"And us," adds Lady Macbeth.

"Yes," Ché adds wryly. "An asterixic assassin, an insomniac with a hand-washing compulsion, a costumed dandy and a punk lesbian with no fixed identity and a bad case of echolalia. Some followers."

"The expropriators are expropriated!" the old man whispers hoarsely.

"Proprieties are appropriated," Suzy chants.

For a moment, the old Librarian appears to regain his senses. He shakes his head, waves a feeble hand and manages another phrase. "Friends... my... never mind an old man... go on ahead."

Clytæmnestra laughs. "O, how he commands! I tremble."

"He's wet his bed again," Lady Macbeth announces.

"Let him lie in it," says Suzy. "What do you care?"

The two older women set to work to clean up the old man, who makes ineffectual attempts to brush away their ministrations while forcing mangled phrases from his throat: "Write Friedrich... mode appropriation... never mind... just an old man... the first negation... individual property... labour... too long the library... too many days..." Suddenly, with surprising strength, he seizes Clytæmnestra's arm. "I've failed... a useless father, despicable husband." Then falling back into his muttering daze: "...capitalist production... inexorable... such high hopes... no money... write Friedrich... its own negation..."

Ché takes a long drag from his gourd of yerba maté. "Ah, remorse, how well I know your poisoned shafts." Passes the bottle to Clytæmnestra. "Remorse is the worm that will eat your flesh."

But what good are recriminations now? Lady Macbeth takes up the mouth organ, slowly, softly, starts up the tango once again. Valentino, drawn out of his brooding by the music, rises, all silk and oil, moves cat-like across the clearing to Clytæmnestra, assumes the position and takes the first step forward into her body. Immediately they're transformed: torsos gliding, feet kneading the ground, two bodies free of the clumsy weight of souls, warm flesh and muscle like a sad thought dancing. Street dance, dance of misery and desire. Broken hearts asleep in Lethe's arms, dreaming in an island of infinity, taking flight from this black city.

"My boots," cries the Librarian.

"Never mind your boots," says Clytæmnestra, breaking off from Valentino and lifting the Librarian from his bed. "Here, I'll help you. Lean on me a little."

> ...te juré que te quería
> mucho más que al alma mía
> y que a mi madre también.

Clytæmnestra drawing the old man close, carrying him through the first tentative steps, the thrust and parry of the cortes, the press of hip to hip, thigh to thigh. The old man clinging to the Queen, vague memories stirring. Clash of steel on steel, a woman's dark eyes, the thick dark stream of Trojan blood. Now the music a little louder. And Guevara's rusted voice.

> Te acoplaste al cotorro
> de este vate arrabalero
> y, te juro hasta diquero,
> por tenerte, se colvió.

Once more Queen and King moving in each other's arms, one last dance for love long gone. Forgotten battles. The city's first story and her last storyteller in the dream of an embrace. Shining telos, sweeping sagas of liberation, le grand soir. A mouthful of wine and pass the bottle on.

Someone's laid a ragged carpet on the ground.

The old man hesitates: "No, no crimson robes. Do not draw the lightning of a jealous God."

"Wash your hands, put on your nightgown; look not so pale," Lady Macbeth taunts the Librarian: "I tell you yet again, Banquo's buried; he cannot come out on's grave." Laughing, she steps into Valentino's waiting arms.

Clytæmnestra, leading the old man through the steps. "Come. A great victor deserves a royal road."

> Se acabaron las versiadas
> de mi numen peregrino,
> si era el verso más divino
> llevarte en mi corazón.

The old man catching on, picking up the pace, the swift double-edged thrust across the ground, bodies pressed together, a single plume of breath rising between them into the dark sky. The moon dancing in the Courtyard of the Dead. Three steps and spin. He, swept up in the play of contradiction, the unity of opposites, negation, while Clytæmnestra unwinds the carpet into the inner chamber. Faster, feet spinning across the ground, too fast, his old heart pounding madly in his ears, his lungs crying out for air, a cloud descending from the rafters, a thousand grasping fingers. The chains of the song like a net — or is that a hammock, they're spinning so fast — tightening round his chest. His head is splitting. A trap. A flash of steel.

"Struck deep — the death blow, deep," shouts Clytæmnestra, swinging a bare hand, full of the memory of a dagger.

As though the blade were real, the old man sinks in her arms, his bloodless lips fluttering. "Socialization…incompatible…at last. Labour… incompatible…the capitalist integument…incompatible…"

> Pensé que fueras el verso
> más intenso de mi vida,
> porque aún sangra la herida
> que tu espiante me causó.

Clytæmnestra carries her partner one more screw's turn into memory. "So he goes down, no way to flee or fight his destiny, the life bursting out of him." There were great sprays of blood, she remembers, a shower dyeing her black and she, she revelling like the Earth under the first spring rain. As though a green spear had split the sheath and ripped her into birth. She, striking, stabbing, and stabbing again, praying for anger to pull her through, for the smoke of hell to fall thick around them, that the knife not see the wound it made, nor heaven peep through the blanket of the dark to cry *Hold, hold!*

The Librarian is falling. "Capitalist production…inexorability…a law of nature…its own…its own…"

"Endless words I've said to serve the moment. How else to prepare a death for deadly men who seem to love you? Done is done. My heart is steel."

"…negation!"

Ya que sabés el secreto
de lo mucho que he sufrido,
decíme quién te ha querido
con más intensa pasión.

The dance pounding in his ears. And then the old men of Argos, so ready to accuse, to banish her from the city, cursing and breathing down her neck. Power, merely the organized power of one class oppressing another. A father sacrificed his daughter, but against him—nothing. Didn't the law demand they banish him?—hunt him from the land for all his guilt? The proletariat…the ruling class never vanquish'd be, until Great Birnham Wood to high Dunsinane Hill, sweep away by force the old conditions… But now they're ruthless judges. Threaten away! I'll meet you blow for blow. Shall come against him. Sweep away the conditions…class antagonism… And if I fall, the throne is yours. Our own supremacy… If God decrees the reverse…as a class…late as it is, old men, you'll learn your place…abolish…

Finally the blur of bodies slows, stops, and the Librarian collapses, crashing into a nearby hammock. Ché cuts off his song and hurries to the old man's aid. No blood. No stabbing. But his friend has suffered a relapse, a stroke. Valentino steps up to lend a hand, untangling the Librarian from the twisted netting and gently laying the limp exhausted body on the ground at the edge of the dying fire's circle. Suzy cradles Clytæmnestra in her arms. Valentino returns to his brooding. Lady Macbeth pockets her harmonica. Ché draws a shot of Ventolin and another line from Lorca: Life is neither noble, nor good, nor sacred.

Le rêve de Clytemnestre

The sun, somewhere the other side of the clouds, has already dropped behind the edge of the mountain to the west of the lookout. A thin gruel of light washes over the city and the river. The moon, already at her post, seems thinner and paler and lower in the sky than yesterday. At the eastern edge, where the plaza begins to curve out over the city, a young white couple stands interlaced. Further along the half circle, a family of African-American tourists jostles for a turn at the binoculars. Clytæmnestra strides past them without a glance and takes her central position on the ramparts.

Her eyes cast their net across the horizon. Searching for a torch. A light. A sign. She stands erect and unblinking. Regal. *Keeping watch on a far shore, caught between growing shadows and shivering wings and her arms of stone.* So still that after a few long moments even the children squabbling to her left fall silent. And then, as always happens at this hour, slowly the inkwell of the city spills into the river and a shadow begins to form where the rim of the earth folds beneath the sky. The shadow grows darker, takes shape. A figure bending over the surface of the river. The bent frame of the writer over the page. Æschylus.

Clytæmnestra waits. Watches. And even as she watches, Æschylus, the poet, the scribe, the watchdog of Athenian order, invents her. The long sweep of Æschylus' pen scratches out her life. Day after day, the black ink of his hand pours into her veins. But now, with the first deadly breath of night, she begins to feel the weight of his eyelids. Because, in his relentless pursuit of progress, his unflagging defense of the rule of men, even the great Æschylus wearies. And as the sea rises to meet the sky, the fog descends and Æschylus sleeps. In that moment of drifting chaos, free of the chains of her creator's mind, her heart takes flight from the black city and Clytæmnestra dreams.

I dream a dancer. How shall I name her? She floats across the black sky of the city stretched out across the page, skips over the shining liquid surface of the river, drawn tight as a dancer's skin, alone, without the knots and straps of a uniform, and barefoot, slipped free from the tight pink shoes of bondage. And turns. Turns slowly upon herself. Slowly. Alone. She dances. Turning away from the gaze of the one who writes her. Turning away from the world, then back into the world. Turns. Returns. Spinning a centrifugal core. Weaving herself. How shall I call her? This dancer spinning so slowly, so gently. She will take lovers when it pleases her, dance over the piled sheets of the earth, wear long scarves and ride in open automobiles. Men will die at her touch. Spinning revolutions. Isadora...

Clytæmnestra spinning. Like a woman who never stops dreaming. Dreaming a woman who dreams herself. Clytæmnestra, invented by Æschylus, imagines Isadora inventing herself. So that even Isadora, this woman who invents herself, is invented by a woman invented by a man. And yet, Isadora Duncan lives, for an instant, in Clytæmnestra's dream, in the spinning web of a long scarf, in the space of Æschylus's dozing.

Then, as Clytæmnestra spins faster and faster, Æschylus shakes his head, wipes the sleep from his eyes, and the moment is gone. The glimpse of Isadora fades and dies. Clytæmnestra, caught in the tangled script of her scarf, falls.

Isadora's dead. And what was her crime? To dance. Alone and unfettered. To die spinning like a wheel wrapped in a scarf of blood. Isadora, Duncan's daughter. Duncan, another father, another king. Pitiful world. Pitiful to live only in the brief batting of a heavy-lidded poet's eye. Pitiful to die spinning in eternity. And pitiful our dreams, to dream a Duncan's daughter. Condemned to dream always of kings. Of fathers. And yet, are we not of women born? Isadora, who was your mother? Have we forgotten her? As I, Clytæmnestra, dreaming of swans, have forgotten my mother, Leda.

She's falling, spinning down faster than ever, her black hair sailing above her head, her robes flying. And shouting, breathless, one after the other, a litany of names: *Sappho, Behn, Christina, Llangollen.*

She writes in the turbid ink of milk and blood. Alone, at night, unwinding the rope that drops her into sleep, she writes carefully, steadily, lovingly. Line following line, curling tongues on the soft sheets of freshly cut pages, reaching out to me, her daughter—a book of caresses. I can touch her skin, I can feel the soft wet nib roll across the clean white sheet. The quill's sharp prick against the smooth grain of parchment. Two graphemes riding up against each other at the margin. Our pores wide open, drunk on purple wine pouring from a tumescent hand.

Murasaki Shikibu, Dickinson, Radclyffe Hall. Stein. Gertrude, writing machine. There is that sharp, craggy face. There are the eyes like grey sea stones, the short thick small strong hands. Hands that can reach under your skin to the long stretched muscles of your thighs. Let me be Alice; write me, Gertrude. Writing. There was an occupation. Act so that there is no use in a centre. A silence is not indicated by any motion. Why is not sleeping a feat why is it not and when is there some discharge when. There never is. There is Gertrude writing Gertrude. There is that caressing. Gliding is not heavily moving. Looking is not vanishing. Laughing is not evaporating. There can be the climax. There can be the same dress. There can be an old dress. There is not the print. There is that smiling. There is the season. There is that where there is not that which is there is what there is which is beguiling. There is a paste. There is that caressing.

At last she falls again. Clytæmnestra, lying on the stones beneath the railing, muttering incantations. *Li Qingzhao, Al-Khansā', Barnes, Woolf. A thousand and one Scheherazades...* At the end of the parapet, the lovers, intertwined, gaze out over the city. The family of tourists scan the horizon, picking out the landmarks. One of the children, a small black girl in a blue-and-white checked dress and a dozen tight little pigtails who has been watching, sees the spinning Queen go down. Quietly, she drifts away from her brothers, her parents. Approaches. Bends over the trembling and exhausted Clytæmnestra, extends a hand, a finger, touches a cheek. Clytæmnestra opens a single eye and exhales an almost inaudible word: "Iphigenia." Immediately the girl's mother is behind her, pulling her back, looking down over her child, uncertain. The family gathers round the body. The man crouches beside Clytæmnestra, asks if she is all right. "Here," he says, "let me give you a hand." Gently he helps her to her feet, away from the edge of the lookout and onto a park bench where she sits down and breathes long deep breaths, surrounded by her family.

Nightfall. The moon is burning. In the darkening sky over the southern horizon blazing serpents leap from its bubbling surface. Suddenly, a great ball of fire comes booming out of the flaming globe toward them. A meteor passes over the city, spilling sparks in all directions, slicing the night in two from the southern shore of the island to the northern forests. Daylight pours through a gash in the sky and floods the city. Then the fiery rocket vanishes behind le Mont-Royal and the sponge of darkness erases all but a faint memory of the event.

The Heaviness of Concrete

Although he can see nothing through the tinted windows, the curving slope of the car's movement tells him they are on a bridge. Neither the driver nor the two men seated in the back seat with him have made any effort to conceal their faces. On the other hand they have not identified themselves properly. They are not the black-suited gorillas he might have expected; instead, their dress is casual—windbreakers and jeans. One of them, who is actually smaller than Le Corbusier, wears thick glasses over eyes like blue buzzers above a mouth like a mail slot. The larger man sports an Expos baseball cap and a potbelly that bounces to the car's motion. As for the driver, Le Corbusier can see a large angry pimple on the back of his neck. Something to remember should he later be required to identify his abductors. He can't really say there's been any rough stuff, other than a hand on his arm outside the library when he hesitated to get in the car at first. It's more a case of creating a context. There's no need to insist. Mainly they have ignored him, engrossed instead in some disagreement over the strength of the throwing arm of some right fielder whose name he has been unable to make out clearly. Le Corbusier is worried about having abandoned his cart and Pilote outside the library. The dog is tied to the handlebars and his teeth are too few and worn down to chew through the rope. He has tried to raise the issue several times, but they are not interested. Finally, Blue Buzzers suggests he shut up.

At the apex of the curve, the car stops. Blue Buzzers swings his door open and pulls Le Corbusier after him. As soon as he steps out of the car he is struck full in the face by the wind and his eyes begin tearing so heavily he can barely see. But he recognizes the pale green tent of sloping steel beams: the Jacques Cartier Bridge. There is no traffic, not a single car going in either direction. They are alone. Have they shut off the road? Expos Cap places his face inches from Le Corbusier's and shouts something, but it's impossible to make out the words in the roar of the wind. They turn him around and guide him to the west railing. The night sky is rushing past all around them. Through his tears he can see the jewel-encrusted city to the right. On the other side, beyond Notre-Dame Island, the dark desolation of the south shore sends a shudder through him.

Expos Cap pushes Le Corbusier closer to the railing. Down through the darkness, he can just make out the white slash of a wave. A sheer drop of a hundred metres. And then the raging current. "Look," he screams back at his companions, "enough is enough; your little joke is no longer funny. Do not force me to report this to the Ambassador."

Either they can't hear him over the wind and water or they don't care. Expos Cap slides his hands under the prisoner's arms and motions to Blue Buzzers to give him a hand.

Le Corbusier feels the fist of fear tighten around his heart. He fumbles in his pocket for the library card: proof of his honourable intentions. Blue Buzzers surveys him cautiously. The card is not there. They could not have taken it; they never searched him: what could they expect to find in a beggar's pockets? Suddenly the image of Clytæmnestra, bidding him farewell at the edge of the clearing, standing close, dark eyes holding his gaze and, although he never felt it then, now the distinct memory of the feel of her hand slipping, one last time, into his pocket. He has no card, no proof of his scholarship.

He abandons his pocket and resumes his frantic mind search. Forget the card, what about the long list of his achievements? Ronchamp, the housing project in Pessac, la Maison Citrohan, Dom-Ino, his publications, the photograph of him with Rockefeller. But one glance at these two insignificant dullards is enough to tell him how completely worthless all that is to him now. But what about Pilote? Waiting, hungry. Yes, well perhaps. For some reason, he suspects the dog's fate might soften their hearts more than his own does. He tries again to raise the issue. Finally, exasperated, Expos Cap releases his hold and steps around to the trunk of the car. The driver releases the lock and Expos Cap leans in to retrieve something heavy and awkward which might be a cloth sack half-full of bones. When he steps around again Le Corbusier realizes it's Pilote the man is carrying in his arms. At first it appears the dog might have suffocated, but probably he just took advantage of the ride to catch a nap, because now, as Expos Cap pauses briefly to show his prize to Le Corbusier, Pilote opens an eye and yawns. Corbu raises his eyes and Expos Cap nods as if to say, "Yes, that's right, your damned dog." Then, in one motion, he steps to the rail and tosses his load over the side. Pilote goes down, ears sailing behind, without so much as a whimper.

For the first time in his life, Le Corbusier is speechless. He is no longer afraid. What he feels is more like regret. The failures. The Voisin Plan, The Palace of Soviets, Mundaneum, Rio de Janeiro. Then he remembers: in his pocket, the canister. He wrenches his arm free from the small man and fumbles, hoping the old woman took Modulor along with the card. But no, there it is, the small metal case. He pulls it out, thrusts it toward his abductors. "Please," he screams, "you must save Modulor." He pries the cap loose, unwinds the first length of tape. "Some day," he shouts, "this will be worth millions." He tries to go on, but the words are swept away as soon as they pass his lips. Expos Cap leans over and takes the object out of Le Corbusier's hand. He studies it briefly, then whips the entire length of the ribbon free and tosses the container over the rail. Le Corbusier manages to grab a section of the tape as it snakes wildly around them. He points to the markings, yells explanations at them. The two men are annoyed, Le Corbusier can see that: it's cold and the damned wind is unbearable. And this guy won't stop yapping. But he must save Modulor. With a sudden burst of desperate energy he shakes loose from their grasp and begins to gather in the tape. Now they are angry. Expos Cap takes hold of Le Corbusier from behind while Blue Buzzers wads a section of ribbon and jams it into the prisoner's mouth. They drag him back to the rail, kicking at his legs to keep him moving. When they release him, the wind blows him straight back at them and they have to heave him over a second time. He is flying, trailing Modulor like a kite tail behind him, screaming his lungs out into the wind. *The safety razor, the briar pipe, the bowler hat…*

He is walking down to the lake. To take his daily swim. The summer sun warm on his back. Skintight black bathing trunks, a clean white towel around his neck. A straight line of birch trees beckons from the other shore. Removes the towel, places it neatly on the grass, steps forward into the cool water, advances slowly, dipping his hands in and rubbing his arms first, then his legs, face, chest. A deep breath and he dives beneath the surface. Swims straight out in a measured crawl, counting the strokes, breathing evenly—three beats below the surface, rotating his head to take a breath, first to the right side, then to the left. Opens his eyes. *The wine bottle, the flask, the column, the ever-sharp pencil...* The light refracted, bent below the uneven surface of the waves. A dark obscurity of shapes, pre-historic creatures of uncertain form. He lengthens his strokes. Wet shining stones below. The lake dreams irregular shapes, emerging and vanishing without warning. Cursed nature, that imperfect artist. His own hands mottled and twisted, erect tensile hairs wafting in the underwater breeze. He forgets his arms, his pace, loses track of his stroke. *The fountain pen, the typewriter, the telephone...* Patterns collapse in the fluidity of the dance. The haunting memory of a primordial world rises to the surface, drawing him down toward the larvae, toads, beasts lying in disorder below. He plunges. Down. Breathing air thick as marmalade. His ears full of the beat of his heart. The water. Still deeper, only a few centimetres from his hand, two tiny sea horses copulating, a viscous ejaculation clouds his vision. For the first time, he is acutely conscious of...what? His body? *The limousine, the laboratory, the hospital, the gymnasium, the monastery...* The water pouring into his lungs. The long stretched layers of tissue and muscle knotted around hard calcine joints in his back where his wings would have sprouted had he been a bird or an angel instead of a diver.

Syntactics of Sex

Clytæmnestra, exhausted from her spell, goes straight to her bunk and lies down. But does not fall asleep. She wonders what is keeping her awake, then realizes. Suzy. She has grown accustomed to the girl's presence. Hovering in the background. Offering a hand. Listening to Clytæmnestra's rememorizing. Where has she gotten to? She wasn't up on the belvedere as usual waiting to pick up the pieces after Clytæmnestra's spell. Has something happened to her in the city? This is the first time Clytæmnestra has found herself worrying about the child. Not that there's any reason to worry. This one can look out for herself. But it's strange that she should not be back in camp. Clytæmnestra cannot remember when she disappeared. And sleep won't come. She struggles to sit up in her hammock, pausing for a moment to let her head settle, and climbs down to the ground. Still weak and dizzy, she picks her way to the cooking area. Not there, nor visiting with anyone else in the camp. Well, that's it then. Probably gone down into the city.

Clytæmnestra decides to relieve herself before returning to her bed. She picks up the machete by Ché's bunk and walks a ways up the path before striking out into the underbrush to a thicket of ostrich ferns between two poplars. Here she digs her hole in the soft ground and lifts her skirts. Then, while she is still crouching and cleaning herself with a handful of moonwort, she hears a whimpering sound that could be a lost child or a groundhog caught in one of her traps down near the path. Quickly she buries her stool and pushes through the ferns toward the sound. A few dozen yards down the slope and through the trees, Suzy is perched on a fallen and petrified oak half-submerged in a muddy slough. Almost as quickly, Suzy turns and spots her. Immediately the younger woman breaks off her crying, swallowing hard and rubbing both hands across her eyes and nose to erase any trace of tears.

Clytæmnestra stops at the base of the fallen trunk where it trails off into a mixture of peat moss and the tresses of dead roots. "There'll be poison ivy in this mess," she says in a matter-of-fact tone.

Suzy shrugs. "I'm immune."

Not without some difficulty, Clytæmnestra climbs up onto the tree. Suzy watches her take careful steps along the beam toward her, but makes no move.

"Well, damn it, child," Clytæmnestra barks, "aren't you going to help?"

Suzy freezes for a moment, surprised, then leans forward with feigned nonchalance and offers a hand. Clytæmnestra settles down close beside her.

Each movement of one of the women on the tree sends ripples like small waves across the surface of the scum pond.

"It's like we were on a beach," Suzy says.

"No," Clytæmnestra shakes her head. "Not a beach. The things that grow here will kill you if you are not careful." Her finger traces a line along the back of Suzy's hand, from her thumb to her wrist.

Suzy, for once, is all restraint. She remains perfectly still, as though she had come across a wild deer and were afraid to startle her.

"All we have," Clytæmnestra whispers, "is the protection of our own skin. An integument. A sheath of paper-thin birch-bark. A slimy warted frog condom. A polished mirror." She pauses, and Suzy hears, or perhaps imagines, a barely audible trilling. *I've got you…under my skin.*

Slipping down from the dry trunk, into the primordial pool. Coming forward. Laboriously, the mud sucking on the soles of our feet, encasing our ankles. Grounded, rooted in the earth, there is no end to our limbs, we are outcroppings in the slough. Coming forward. Two surfaces rubbing against each other, un frottement, we are semipermeable. *That old black magic that I know so well.* If I enter this wet clearing which is not a swamp but which is dangerous…viscous, how will we emerge? The surface of my self. The thin dry surface of your hand, a milky white phrase curling like birch-bark from the tree, the damp centre of my transitive palm on your soft inner thigh, the dark ellipsis, the callused heel, the future perfect eye. A bone, a nail, a soft cedilla. An ætatis. Moving into each other like the sea leaking back into a river, rain beating the surface of a pond, water breaking into memory. My dreams. Then, the steady dry thumping of two fingers on a tightly stretched tympani, beating out a song, but not a steady rhythm, that would be too easy, no, the meter fluctuates somewhere the other side of reassurance, the light thrill of an erratic pulse. *I've got you under my skin.* The way a cat keeps a list of hiding places buried somewhere deep inside the cortex: under the table, beneath the bed, between the wall and the stove, on top of the bookshelf, inside the drawer left open just a crack. I've been over this ground. In my memory. There is a blurring of boundaries …between us…between me…between the eyes looking, the words. A copulative conjunction, a diagonal slash, a double dagger. The passage of your eye over the ground burning an imprint on my mind. *That old black magic that we know so well.* You are the fold in the surface of the pond, the lip of the wave. The ablative absolute.

Son of Sheik

In the late evening Rudy abandons Ché's radio spread in pieces across the ground and slips away. He has always loved tinkering with machinery, but so often the pleasure seems to wear off before the parts come back together. (On that final visit with Natasha to the Château Juan les Pins in Nice, her stepfather in a huff, finally forced to call in the expert from England to reassemble the electric piano. Was that how he'd lost her? His failure to make things whole again?) In any case, as far as the radio goes, it's no use; he will have to make it up to Guevara somehow later. For now, he feels the pull of a different desire. To shed this skin. To be reborn. A hero. Riding across the sand, untamed, the fearless lover. Purged of his failures. Jean Acker: her disappointment. Three days of marriage, then divorce, and the word *unconsummated* on everyone's lips. Even before that, Blanca de Saulles: under the heel of her battering pig of a husband; Rudy'd sworn to save her, but the husband had sent his goon—just a threat, the back of a hand across his face—and she finally had to shoot the pig herself. And of course Natasha, gone, to find…herself. His mother, Donna Gabriella. Rodolpho, you have disgraced our name. Hadn't he defended her name with his fists? How many boys had he beaten when they refused to admit her beauty? Even so, she had turned him out, banished him an ocean away…until you can bear our name with pride…the name he'd shed in the debris of the harbour.

In the Chalet washroom, he lays out the long white sheet he has borrowed from Clytæmnestra's bunk and strips off his gaucho costume. Painstakingly, he remakes himself in clean white cotton robes, stringed beads, headgear, until finally, there, standing like a dark mystery in the mirror above the sink: the figure of The Sheik.

Only the finishing touches remain: a drop of blood from his finger to redden the lips, a touch of cinder to the eyes. He bends toward the glass to test a few close-ups—the lover's gaze, the savage leer, the regal pose, the slow blink of innocent charm, the glance of a stranger across the room, contempt, defiance, unacknowledged suffering, the bravely born pain of mortal injury —all there, still intact, still flawless, wordless silence speaking volumes.

A presence in the doorway. Ché, staring. Rudy drops the mask, turns to face the Argentinian and that look of half surprise, half disgust. "You, on the other hand," Rudy says tightly, "could do with a change of clothes, or at least a bath."

Ché looks him up and down, shakes his head slowly, hesitates, search-ing for the right approach. "You wrecked the radio."

Rudy shrugs. "I'll buy you another one."

Today's *Tribune* on the breakfast tray by his bed, opened and neatly folded to the editorial page. *A new public ballroom was opened on the north side a few days ago, a truly handsome place and apparently well-run.*

"Never mind. You might just as well go."

The pleasant impression lasts until one steps into the men's washroom.

Rudy laughs. "What, too many recruits?"

"Quantity is not my primary concern. We have no need of…"

"What?"

A powder-vending machine! In a men's washroom! Homo Americanus!

"The guerrilla fighter," Ché undertakes calmly, "as the conscious element of the popular vanguard, must display a moral conduct that does credit to a true priest…"

"Go on, say it. No need of what?" Rudy grinds through clenched teeth.

"…a true priest of the reform which he seeks."

How does one reconcile masculine cosmetics, sheiks, floppy pants, and slave bracelets…

"To the austerity imposed by the difficult conditions of war, he must add the austerity born of a rigid self-control which precludes even a single excess, a single slip, no matter if circumstances permit it."

Do women like the type of 'man' who pats pink powder on his face in a public washroom? Hollywood is the national school of masculinity.

On the wall, some sort of apparatus: vending machine? hand dryer? Rudy turns to the wall, takes hold of the machine with both hands. It so happens I am sick of being a man.

Rudy, the beautiful gardener's boy, is the prototype of the American male.

In a single powerful movement he rips the hand dryer out of the wall, heaves it into the cubicle, exploding the porcelain urn and releasing a geyser of turbid water.

The editorial entitled *PINK POWDER PUFFS.*

Ché steps quickly out of the way of the gushing liquid. "Are you mad?" he shouts. Rudy, standing now in a growing puddle, has slipped into silent defiance — head bent slightly forward, eyes glaring fiercely, fists clenched stiffly by his sides. Beginning of the second reel.

Outside, a police siren is faintly yawping.

Ché shifts into battle mode. "We'd better clear out. You take the stairs downtown. I'll go by the camp and warn the others." He hesitates a moment, waiting for Valentino to move. "Come on, Rudy," he shouts, sloshing toward him. They are separated by the brown water cascading from the cubicle. "You've got to get out." He can hear the cop car bawling, see the dust twister climbing up the road. No time to lose. Ché steps out the door. The blue-and-white is already in view. He turns back once more into the flooding room, shouts a final warning and vanishes into the brush.

It is time for matriarchy if the male of the species allows such things to persist. Better a rule by masculine women than effeminate men. Why didn't someone quietly drown Rodolpho Guglielmi, alias Valentino, years ago?

It's a Dog's Life

On and on, this one struggles, legs straining to break the plane of water, to maintain this one's head above the surface where breathing is possible but no, not easy, a mouth full of water and no scent, not merely no sign of the others but no scent at all, nothing but the taste of bad water, and straining to keep this one's head above water, now that this one has been separated from the others, the one that speaks gone, standing in dehiscent mutism on the bridge, the memory of the dark enclosure rocking this one to sleep and then the raging wind, a full-blown hyperborean blast confusing everything in a salmagundi of odours, and this one in the arms of that other one tasting of unripe fruit, but that was before the long descent and now that this one is alone the thing is to continue straining to maintain this one's head high above the rolling walls of speckled miasma though there is no scent, no sign of the First One, nor even of the one who speaks, not a whiff of deciduous tang nor steaming pungency, nothing, so that this one is alone and desires only to find the others, the First One in the den, the soft putrefaction in the warm spot beside the First One's sleeping place, to escape this terrible inodorous void, this complete lack of information, this darkness...

And then finally a hint of tartness, a vague astringency, and something solid striking this one's left front paw: the shore, onto which this one scrambles over slippery rock, through rancid vegetation, up onto the berm along the moiré's edge, and now this one is safely out of the river, the weight of exhaustion and the bone-chilling cold take over, the uncontrollable trembling begins; legs, like rubber bones, refuse to stack up straight beneath this one's body, but there is no time to lie down or rest, to bury this one's snout in a delicately fetid accumulation of debris over there by the wire fence, no time because, before anything else, this one must find the First One, return to where this one belongs, to the pack and leave this terrible thing that has happened behind—terrible not so much because of the long fall, the freezing water, the brutal waves, but because of the singularity of the experience, because this one has undergone it alone, apart from the group, and for this one or any one in this dog's world can there be any salvation apart from the group? No, none, no salvation, so onward, pausing only long enough to snort the water from this one's nose before beginning the long and arduous search back to the den, a search that will require all this one's thankfully prodigious hunting skills, a proficiency of which this one remains on the whole confident in spite of the fact that this one is long past antediluvian, not to mention toothless and tired, still this one's olfactory powers are intact, and even now, there, not far away, this one can make out the unmistakably familiar redolence of another dog's shit.

Hwe-do-ne-e-e-eh?

First, a tinkling sound. Like tiny crystal tambourines. Rain drops shivering in the trees. Standing in the midst of traffic on Sainte-Catherine, de Maisonneuve stares along the divided length of McGill College Avenue, between Place Montréal-Trust on one side and the Eaton Centre on the other, over the old stone archway at the entrance to the university and up beyond the green campus. For one frozen instant, it's all there: a line of crosses rocking on the curling crest of Mount Royal, two small threads of blood splitting the hard sky and, in the air above the shuddering crosses, standing immaculately white upon the quarter moon, the Virgin of Sorrows, seven daggers planted in her heart. And then, just as quickly, the street has slipped out from under him, forcing him to his knees and knocking the crucifix from his shoulders. A gradual roar rises up from the throat of the earth.

People are pouring out of the shops and banks into a street full of police sirens, hysterical church bells and screaming heads full of night and excrement and trembling little girls. Walls, beams, joints and boards crack, roofs bend in every direction, all the stones are in motion. "Speak, Lord," de Maisonneuve whispers, shutting his eyes: "speak with the utterance of thunder and earth quaking."

Let the earth leap up and the palisades dance. Let the mountains wage war, rising up and hurling themselves at each other. Let yawning chasms appear where mountains once stood, fling trees out of the ground and replant them in forests of upturned trunks and roots grasping wildly at the air. Split the ice on the river into a million fragments and spew clouds of smoke and jets of mud and sand. Let the stink of sulphurous water rise from a thousand springs, and the rivers run red. Send lances of fire down from the sky to enflame the houses. Fill the night with voices of lamentation, the wailing of children, the cries of women, the prayers of men kneeling in the snow.

Hwe-do-ne-e-e-eh? When will this come to pass?

Then suddenly it's over and the earth is still. The rain has stopped. And in the brief silence that precedes like a single long breath the din of rescue and grief, a white sword of wind sweeps across the city and fills de Maisonneuve with doubt. Strange that he should falter only moments after such a powerful demonstration of a supernatural presence, but the physical sensation of the ground moving beneath his feet has somehow made certainty of any kind impossible, at least as long as the memory of the earth's betrayal remains fresh in his mind.

And there are fires. He can smell the brownish smoke, hear the sirens. And the voices again, louder than ever. *Hwe-do-ne-e-e-eh?* He opens his eyes, which have been closed since the quake hit. In the shattered glass of Place Montréal-Trust, de Maisonneuve sees, again, the face with eyes full of intelligence and strength he knows is not his own.

The face of the one whose name must not be spoken, the one whose face Aionwahtha the man-eater saw reflected in the surface of his hearth pot. The Peacemaker.

The mountain has grown, thrust by the quake up and over the city, so that it now curves like the heel of some menacing boot, and there, still standing at the apex, bigger than ever: the cross, his cross, burning in a sheath of blood-red flames.

Ha! Ha! Hail! Hail! Hail! We bring the wishes of the Great Peace. Kaianereh'kowa: The Great Law, The Way of Great Splendour. Gaiwoh: justice and the desire for justice. Skenon: the peace which comes when the spirit is healthy and the body is cared for. Gashasdenshaa: the strength to apply justice and the will of the Creator.

Who are you?

We are Kanien'keha:ka, the people of the Land of Flint.

We are Rotinonhsion:ni, the people of the Long House, the Great Peace, the Circle of Life.

We are Wisk Nihohnohnwenstiake, the Five Nations.

We are Kanonsionnionwe, the League of the Long Houses.

Onkwehonwe. We are the people come together.

Hwe-do-ne-e-e-eh? Atotarho's incredulous question. To win Atotarho's support for the project of the Five Nations was the Peacemaker's first great challenge. Atotarho, cruel sorcerer, his spirit twisted seven times, his body twisted seven ways, and his head covered in tangled snakes, sitting on his great rock in the Onandagan Valley, striking birds dead out of the sky with a single wave of his arm and devouring all who dared to appear uninvited before him. Atotarho, closing his ears to the message of Great Peace, unbelieving, taunting: *And when will this come to pass?*

People stagger past de Maisonneuve like shipwrecked survivors. His cross lies before him, split in two and encased in a sheet of flame. A belt of burning beads. *Tekeniteyoha:te, the Two-Row Wampum, the Treaty of Two Paths.*

Two parallel lines. Two ships running down the length of the river. On one side, the swift, silent canoe of the Five Nations; on the other, the great white sails filled with the crack of falling trees. Each vessel moving freely on the water, each people living freely in its own way. This was the agreement, the Silver Chain of Alliance, l'Alliance des bras levés: never to cross the other's path, never to impede the other's progress.

But now white sails career crazily over the width of the river, crashing into the birch-bark canoes. Two paths are crossed. And two crossed sticks mark the summit above Tiontiakwe, the place the white men call Montréal. This cross, this sign with which the white man marks the places where he buries his dead. Signs of vengeance and murder. The mountainside covered with these signs of the dead. The black stink of death covering the city. Blood flows down the mountainside from the sign of the double cross and washes over the land. The great river runs red.

Are white people unable to stand two sticks straight in the ground? Must the Rotinonhsion:ni show them how, as they taught them where to fish and how to grow maize and store food for the winter? For the Kanonsionni existed and were operating before white people arrived in this country. One day, the people of Great Peace will show white people The Great White Pine and the white roots of peace.

Asonke-ne-e-e-e-eh? Has it not yet come to pass?

In the haze of tears, he feels a familiar tug on his sleeve. Pilote, returned from the dead, soaking wet and stinking to high hell, has found him somehow in all the chaos. And to make matters worse, the dog has waited until now to shake himself off. The terrible stench kicks the clouds out of de Maisonneuve's head. But he has barely enough time to shove the animal away and scramble to his feet before the cops are on him. They must have been after the ragged dog. Cleaning up in disaster's aftermath. There's no time to put up any resistance. Suddenly there are no signs of the earthquake's damage, no smoke or wreckage, no cross or flames or voices; he is alone inside the windowless blue van, a broken soldier with his stinking dog.

Ché Lives!

A blue paddywagon parked at the top of the Peel Street hill. That should have been warning enough. But by the time he picks up all the signs, they're approaching Sherbrooke and it's too late; they're in too deep, the ambush is sprung. A platoon of uniforms sweeping up from the south while the plainclothes come down from Pine. Luckily the Peruvian street musicians in front of the bank are putting up some resistance, using their flutes to ward off the assault, which provides a few precious seconds for Ché to shuffle the old Librarian through the alley behind the Student Union building and onto the campus of the university. Here the meandering path through clean green spaces, the pale stone buildings and the soft patter of the Three Bares Fountain seem to promise sanctuary. But, while it's true that, two or three decades ago, they could have counted on student militancy to keep the police off campus, these days they are more likely to encounter joint patrols. So Ché ignores the Librarian's tugging suggestion to sit a while and steers him quickly into the library.

Today's newspaper, splayed across a table in the reference section, confirms his worst fears. Below the screaming headline — "Chalet Toilets Destroyed in Suicide Bombing. Arab Terrorists Suspected" — a head-and-shoulders of Rudy in sheik headdress.

"We had better lie low awhile," Ché decides.

Of course, splitting his forces was a mistake. He can admit that now, just as he must finally accept that Joaquin and the others are dead. A sun that melted the stones. That morning, in his diary, he had written a single word: *Defeat.*

The Librarian's job is gone, but they have something else for him. And for Ché, if he wants it. The idea is not without its merits. From his earliest travels with Albert Granados across the Americas to the Granma expedition, the Congo and, of course, Bolivia, his has always been a life of action (the demands of his era, "the time of the furnaces" as Martí put it), yet a part of him has always regretted the reflective life, the quiet solitude of scholarship, the severe dedication, the womb-like timelessness of the library. In fact, a job here is, he suddenly realizes, exactly what he wants, what he has always wanted. Temporarily.

Whatever the reason—something about removing or relocating certain books on the shelves—they need help urgently; the application form is so undemanding he barely has to lie at all.

And the Librarian seems rejuvenated; he takes a deep breath of the stale air and begins to move toward the familiar ground of the reference section. But there's no time for that. A short squat woolly lady takes charge of them. To Ché, she is a typical product of the library: spectacles riding on a shelf of breasts that render the gold chain superfluous, and that way of pronouncing all her consonants perfectly through tight red lips. Nevertheless, for someone starting out in a new job, it is somehow comforting to be addressed as 'dear', to breathe in the grandmotherly aroma of thickly layered face powder. She leads the two men through a door at the rear of the reception area and down a winding metal staircase which might be a fire escape except that it is indoors and walled in. She leads the way, spiraling down and down into the intestines of the library. Once in a while they encounter small tight landings, but there seem to be no doors; of course, it's difficult to tell, as the mildewed walls grow progressively dimmer. Eventually he can barely find the steps or maintain sight of the woollen sweater. He hears the Librarian puffing behind, but he can do nothing to help; he is too involved with feeling his own way, listening for the clinking of their guide's heels on the metal stairs and sniffing for her powdery scent through the stink of mildew. Then he feels her hand take his and squeeze firmly and he reaches back to do the same for his old friend, and the three continue their descent that way in a kind of broken kindergarten ring.

Finally they come to a halt and his hand is released. He can hear her struggling with a door, groping for a light switch. By now he has lost track of the number of flights they have come down, as well as any hope of re-emerging. He only prays there might be a cot and some food to keep them going until the job, whatever it might be, is done. The light, when it comes on at last, does nothing to reassure him: a single long fluorescent tube blinking on and off in a high ceiling. They stand for a moment in the door, their upturned faces waiting for the tube to finally break off stuttering and fulfill its promise. But it only flickers incoherently until Ché has to lower his eyes. The room is a vast storage space, flooded with brown cardboard boxes. Here and there a box has burst and spilled brand new texts onto the dirty cement floor. Books sprawl in unnatural postures, some of them offering up their glossy white interiors to the inhospitable surroundings. Looking at a pile close by, he can see the marks of grease and smudged footprints across a page.

Saturday, October 7. The eleventh month of operations in Bolivia. The canyon of Quebrada del Yuro, when we first came upon it, seemed like an end to our troubles. A good place for an ambush. There were potato plants watered by ditches so that, at last, we could quench our thirst and quell our pangs of hunger.

"Here we are, then," the woolly lady sings in her most cheerful pre-school voice.

His ears are blocked, as though they were underwater. The supervisor leads them through the corrugated badlands. In the far corner of the room, emerging from a spot high in the wall, where one might have hoped for a window, is the end of a tin chute.

She glances round at the hills of boxes, which are particularly plentiful in this area, and back up at the chute. "I do hope you'll be all right," she says, pursing her lips and eyeing the Librarian, who has found a soft mound of books to sit on. Clearly, she would like Ché to reassure her. He, on the other hand, wants more information.

"Oh, of course," she says. "I'm sorry, dear. The books. The books come down from…that." She gestures quickly toward the mouth gaping in the wall above them and her voice drops slightly. "You catch the boxes and pile them there," she says, nodding vaguely in the direction of the room beyond.

There is no visible order to the stacks of boxes, aside from the larger quantity of wreckage in the vicinity of the chute. Either there has been some sudden and terrible textual catastrophe or their predecessor (or predecessors) was left alone to gradually degenerate into apathy before being fired. Obviously the library does not much care; these must be the books they have decided to clear off the shelves for some reason. Why?

To make room for new and better volumes? Because they are in some way dangerous, offensive, out of fashion? Because they have been too long on the shelves without attracting new readers? There's no way of knowing. The supervisor does not wish to discuss it. Ché senses she is waiting for some sign from him to release her, some evidence of his having minimally understood their task so that she can leave this place. She has begun to fidget as though her sweater were infested.

He does not want her to go, not yet. "Should we stack the books in alphabetical order?" he asks.

"If you like," she says absently.

He could keep her there by asking about the hours, lunch and breaks or the salary—all questions any self-respecting employee should have at his or her fingertips—but his mind has gone blank, so they stand smiling uneasily at each other until, finally, she moves away, gaining speed as she puts distance between them. Then the door slams and she's gone, leaving them alone with the stammering light and the chute. Ché looks over at his companion, who is staring up at the hole. The hole stares back with the mindless hungry look of a shark. Together, the half-wit light, the hole, and the two men wait. It occurs to Ché that they are surrounded by books, just as he has always longed to be, but instead of embracing them, he feels as though he ought to be building a fire to keep them at bay.

Of course, it was the old lady who gave them away, the one they had spotted grazing her goats on the hillside. It was basic military procedure to detain any civilians encountered before an engagement. In case of informants. Normally, Ché would have detained her, at least until they were safely out of the canyon. Why then, this time, had he let her go? She stopped walking when she saw them. But she showed no fear, did not run. He halted the column. They stood still like that for many long moments, the guerrillas and the old woman watching each other from a distance. She seemed to be looking straight at him. Her face was expressionless, but Ché read the betrayal in her eyes. Perhaps he knew it no longer mattered. It was only a matter of time. *Defeat.* Finally she had turned her back on him and he heard the tinkle of bells as the goats followed her out of the canyon.

A low growling sound coming from somewhere up above, deep in the chute's throat, grows gradually louder. Ché places himself under the hole.

The noise becomes a roar, then a screech, and a box swings out of the dark mouth of the chute, hanging free in the air for an instant before falling straight down on Ché's solar plexus and kicking all the air out of him. His knees buckle, the box continues on its way, crashing into the ground and bursting open like a Christmas cracker. His lungs desperately sucking in chunks of dusty air, he staggers back a few steps and sinks to his knees. Slowly, the books ooze out of their shattered cardboard shell, beautifully bound volumes of something called *The Golden Ass* fanning out in a semicircle around him.

While he is still down on all fours fumbling for his Ventolin, the shark begins to growl again. The Librarian scrambles to his feet to lend a hand, but Ché pushes him back and moves into the dark spot below the mouth of the chute. Another roar and screech and a second box flies out at him. This time he takes it high on the chest and manages to hang on long enough to cushion the fall. Immediately, more growling. Ché swings around to set the carton down as quickly as possible, but by the time he has turned back to the chute the next box is on him, hitting him squarely on the shoulder before smashing into the cement.

"Wait!" he shouts up into the mouth of the chute, in case someone on the other end might hear. The chute roars back and spits another box. Ché steps back and lets this one crash into the pile. Two more cartons follow in rapid succession, but he is out of the line of fire now, his useless arms dangling by his rubbery knees, his heart squeezing with each collision, as he watches the boxes go, like lemmings, to terrible destruction.

A pause. No more books. But something else—a low roar gradually building in the chute, a sound like dogs barking. The ground begins to tremble. At first he tells himself it's only his dizziness, but the Librarian is hanging on to an oversized box of world atlases for dear life. The whole room is shaking. The ceiling light flickers madly. The barking grows louder, becomes a deafening howl, and a greenish wind stinking of rotting fruit and paper dust pours from the mouth of the chute into the room. He remembers Neruda: "an empty shoe, an empty suit of clothes, a barking where there are no dogs." He's forgotten the rest of it. Then the deliveries begin again. This time there are no boxes: only a rapid fire of individual books. Ché, spurred on for a moment by the variation, makes a fresh attempt to save a few, but after a dozen futile stabs and a hard edge to the forehead, he retreats to the Librarian's side. Still the books keep coming. The two men are forced back as the piling books crest and roll toward them. Ché fights to stay afloat. He tries to grab the old man, but they are separated by volumes. Another wave breaks over them. The room is filling up. Breathing is becoming impossible. He manages to extricate the Ventolin from his pocket but immediately it is snatched away by a crosscurrent. He was wounded in the leg. "Do not shoot," he told the captain, "I am Ché Guevara." Then the asthma takes over and he can say no more. There's nothing to do but swim and hope the flow of books breaks off before they are pounded to death or drowned. The weedy scent of the lake, the cold water, the dark grasses swinging back and forth in the current, his mother's hair, damp and falling over her bare shoulders as she bends toward him with the outstretched towel. "Come, Teté, you'll catch cold." And the first cough pressing against his chest, the first handshake of the asthma that would become his lifelong companion.

A Vague Astronomy of Shapeless Pistols

As soon as they step into the clearing, Suzy knows something is wrong. In the aftermath of the quake, the camp has been abandoned. Only Lady Macbeth remains, scavenging through the debris one last time on her way out. Another of Ché's false alarms? Apparently not. Something has gone wrong up at the Chalet. The woods are full of men.

"Arm, arm, and out! Ring the alarm bell! There is no tarrying here."

Clytæmnestra gathers her hammock of netting and a few things and the women file down the secret animal paths toward the east.

Three figures emerge from the woods at the foot of the mountain, pausing on the long grassy slope overlooking Park Avenue. Beyond the eight lanes of high-speed traffic, Parc Jeanne-Mance stretches for another two blocks, as though the mountain were leaking back into the city. A soccer field, tennis courts and a ragged pick-up game of baseball which proceeds religiously in spite of the line of paddywagons along the third-base line. Blue uniforms dot the outfield.

Suzy takes the lead. Slightly dizzy, the heady mix of imminent danger and that delicious twinge in your stomach that comes from resisting the urge to turn and take Clytæmnestra's hand. Even though you know today at last you could if you wanted to. Could walk arm in arm through the park. Let your hand slide on her hip. Look straight into her eyes. Could. If you wanted to. And you do. Want to. But you choose not to. Choose instead to defer the pleasure. Striding ahead, down to the Marie-Anne Street crossing, past the children's playground, between the football and soccer fields to a large four-storey…but no, the times we live in, neither the house nor its location can be revealed. Imagine something like a convent, but unmarked. An unnamed order? Sisters in clandestinity? Suzy knows the place; she's been here before, though she only vaguely remembers why. She rings, submits to an intercom interrogation, and the trio waits several moments on the doorstep, casting anxious glances into the park, before they are finally granted entry.

The women have gathered in the main hall, a long empty room lined with mirrors and exercise bars, for their daily self-defense class. They are all here (or so it might seem, though many more are missing): Isadora in her loose white robes and bare feet, Sappho leaping jetés across the floor, Emily diligently practising pliés at the bar, Virginia brooding in the corner out of range of the mirror, and a dark figure off to the side, perhaps Al-Khansā'? And Gertrude, feet planted squarely on the hardwood floor, Joan, Théroigne de Méricourt, Gabriela Silang, Camille, Tekakwitha, Sojourner Truth, Rosa… And in the centre, between the mirrors, Clytæmnestra, demonstrating, a thousand and one times, her technique with net and dagger.

Across the road, across the fields and forests, the war rages on. Somewhere beyond the river Aulis. But here, there's lunch in the common kitchen and washing up, math problems in the study room, a breath of air and a good book on the terrace, a long talk by the fire. Verses and the clean sweat of hard work. Clear voices and soft hands. These are the years between the reigns of Agamemnon and Orestes. Years unmarked on any calendar. Clytæmnestra's kingdom. Here even Lady Macbeth might feel safe. For a while. Except that the secret is out. Already a line of placards has formed in the street out front. Stop Discrimination. Justice for Men. No Tax Dollars for Shelters. The Male Victims' League. Fathers' Union for Custody Rights. The Canadian wing of the Fathers' Alliance for Liberty in the United States. From the top-floor windows, Lady Macbeth watches the forest of pickets advancing on the gates of their fortress. She can hear the rage building. Strangely, the police are gone from the park. Vanished. Luckily there is a back way out. Most of the women are already slipping out into the alley, and dispersing to the east. Gone Isadora, Catherine Tekakwitha, Saint Joan, mademoiselle Claudel, brave Gabriela. Sojourner down to the train station, Sappho to the cliffs, Virginia toward the river, Rosa by the bridge. All of them, gone.

Walking along the narrow Duluth Street sidewalk, Suzy and Clytæmnestra are too preoccupied with sidestepping dog dirt and taking in the magazine display in the side windows of the lime-green building on the corner of Saint-Laurent to notice the commotion ahead until they find themselves suddenly on The Main and swept up in the swarming crowd. Masses of people jamming both sidewalks and edging out over the curbs, pushing to get a better view of the procession. What is it? Parade? Protest? Spontaneous uprising? Wedding? Funeral procession? Impossible to tell from the marching formations; one moment filing by in ordered rows, the next leaping and running in a chaos of arms and howling faces. They come in small groups, by the thousands, two by two, all alone, on foot, on bicycles, posing atop a hundred allegorical floats. They march as the Actors' Guild, the major film studios, the Italo-American and Canadian federations, politicians of every stripe, the YWCA, the SPCA, the AAA, the Cultural Studies Association, the Gay and Lesbian Rights Coalition. Men in dark suits and fresh haircuts, black-shawled women, Shriners, gum-chewing schoolgirls, mascaraed flappers, trim socialites, gorgeous brilliant-plumed transvestites, drugstore sheiks, gauchos, toreros, James Deans, Marilyn Monroes, punks, bodybuilders, leather lovers. Eighty thousand mourners—parading, blowing horns and whistles, chanting slogans, wailing and crying and fainting and tearing their clothes. Someone hands Suzy a monogrammed cigarette and an eight-by-ten glossy of The Sheik. Full figure.

Finally the casket comes into view. Rudolph Valentino, riding high atop a black limousine, in the open coffin on a bed of roses, his head resting on a scarlet cushion. Mourners carrying wreaths, including one from Mussolini himself, surround the car. Directly behind the hearse, the official party: Pola Negri, leaning on George Ullman's arm and swooning at the awful sight of her lover (even though the talk is nothing ever happened). Ullman grim-faced and silent, calculating the cost of the funeral against the returns. Here, at last, as they reach the Bistro Quatre, he comes to the end of subtracting from the half-million dollar Valentino debt and takes his first step into the gilded realm of addition. Film rights, advertising contracts, perfumed contributions from broken-hearted dowagers, all piling up toward what will turn out to be a $600,000 balance in the estate.

Rudy's back. Good old George's done it again. We're back on tour. Only this time, no $7000 a week, no Falcon Lair waiting for your return, no English cigarettes monogrammed in gold, no fancy suits and slave bracelets. No tango. No Natasha. Now it's twelve minutes past midnight and a bad case of peritonitis. Still, Rudy's back on tour. Riding down to the old port. The ships docking on the pier. The crowds. The day he set foot on the quay at New York. Homeless. The streets crowded with sweeping mobs of people. And Rodolpho being carried along, that peculiar sinking feeling, like a man in the middle of an ocean—wave upon wave of strange faces uttering strange sounds.

Suzy elbows some room for a closer look, almost trampling a small boy in ragged jeans too big for him. The kid is selling newspapers, a special edition, with a front-page full-colour photo of the cortège that has to have been taken a good half day before the funeral. Good old George. Suzy has time to make out the words *RIOT* and *DEATHS* in the headline before the boy is swept past her. She turns to take Clytæmnestra's hand.

"Look out for yourself," the Queen says harshly, patting her once on the rump and pushing her away before stepping back into the mass of loose pockets and dangling purses. "I work alone."

The police attack in a phalanx of two hundred riot shields and gas masks. On foot, on motorcycles, waving long nightsticks, firing tear gas and rubber bullets. The crowd pushes and folds in on itself. Unsure which way to run, people go down under the heels of their neighbours. "Threaten away!" shouts Clytæmnestra, slipping her knife into her free hand. "I'll meet you blow for blow. If I fall the throne is yours."

Suzy is swinging her elbows and knees just to keep afloat, not even thinking of the pigs; the crowd has become the enemy. Until a dark scent of leather tells her they are very near. The crowd thins, the faces all turned in the same direction. And then they're there, a black line of smoked glass and amphibian skulls. It's the boots she smells, shining patent leather stretched tight over steel. The line advances efficiently, rhythmically, like threshers in a wheat field. Black rubber, black leather, leaden skulls. Suzy pulls to free herself from the clutch of bodies, but she cannot reach Clytæmnestra. Clytæmnestra stepping into that space the length of a nightstick which always forms like an invisible membrane between the police and a retreating crowd. Her right arm gently traces an arc in the dead air, she raises a hand, peering through her fingers at the dark masks. The line slows. Hesitates. Bends around her. Slowly she turns once on her heel. "Let's go," Suzy says and whispers her name. The troops pause, standing perfectly still, only their sticks jiggling nervously on their hips. Suzy, outside the circle, probes for an opening. Nothing. Clytæmnestra's left hand emerges from the folds of her robe and the dagger winks in the reflected light of a hundred shields. I hear the creaking of leather soles as the men shift onto the balls of their feet. Clytæmnestra leans forward, taps the tip of her blade against the jet-smooth surface of the nearest shield. Spins slowly away.

Orestes, is it you? Come at last to restore your father's reign? I see murder in your eyes. Come, Orestes, come, the snake I bore. The hounds of a mother's curse will hunt you down. Come silence Clytæmnestra. The light is breaking. Time strides through the gates of our house, and the iron boot of history once more advances, inexorable, grinding everything in its path into the same fine sand. Well, come on then, do it and be done.

The circle tightens. Suzy cries out. A gloved fist throws her roughly back and off her feet. She scrambles up to catch a glimpse. Clytæmnestra's black hair spinning above the helmets. A chorus of nightsticks.

Once More, Ophelia

A top the women's shelter, a figure in a nightgown paces to and fro. Rubs her hands, muttering as she sleepwalks from one edge of the roof to the other. East or west, wherever she turns her gaze, the same thin gloss of blood covers everything. Blood to the west, over grey Mount Royal's cross, the grey slopes, the muddy park and the forest of placards pouring through the shelter's gates. Blood to the east, over her sisters scurrying into the back alley, over the funeral procession sweeping down boulevard Saint-Laurent, the slanted tower of the Olympic Stadium and the angry river. What is it about this blood that makes her crazy? Not merely the fact of blood, but rather its consistency. Shimmering and beading over everything. If only it were a thick crimson or royal blue, or even the dry brown crusted blood of remorse, but no, this is a watery pink gloss, the blood of small animals, of squirrels and sparrows, the blood of an old man. While at last, after too many centuries, Birnham Wood finally advances, coming in rows of trees, steaming breath and dragging their tangled roots behind them. At last, even in her sleep, her hands spotted, her gown stained, pacing across her rooftop, Lady Macbeth knows there is neither flying hence nor tarrying here. At last, she has had enough. Panhandling on street corners, huddling around stinking subway grates, forever looking over her shoulder for the next attacker. Waiting in a sleepless room of cold stones for the advancing forest of enemies to tighten its grip on her dreams. Now, at last, she is finally weary of the moon, tired of the world.

She steps forward to the edge of the roof in plain view of the crowd below. Slowly, she draws the blade from the folds of her gown, turns it in her hand, against her breast, and then, in one swift movement, plunges it into her heart. O happy dagger! This is thy sheath; there rest, and let me die. One long deep breath, to feel one last time the cold air fill her lungs, and she takes that single step over the edge. Floating rags fluttering in time and space and then down, down, down. She's standing, for the first time, naked in the open air, white serpents curled about her ankles, the sun, the breeze beating upon her, and the waves inviting. She pushes forward, walks out, her arms stroking through the cold surface of the sea. The soft, cold embrace of the ocean. On and on. Don't look back. The bluegrass meadow of her childhood, with neither beginning nor end. On and on. Her arms grown heavy, her legs tired. "The artist must possess the courageous soul that dares and defies." Exhaustion pressing in. Until at last, the shore far behind and her strength gone, the old terror flames up for an instant, and she sinks again. Her father's voice. Her sister's. The barking of an old dog somewhere on the shore. The spurs of the cavalry officers. The hum of bees and the musky odour of pinks filling the air. Rosemary for remembrance, pansies, fennel and columbine. Withered daisies and violets. And now your sister's drowned. Floating on the water's surface. Flying east to the Olympic Stadium's slanting tower and plunging into the willow's image in the stream. Floating awhile on the raft of her wild dress — crowflowers, nettles and long purples — spread wide on the surface of the brook, and singing, hey nonny, nonny, until her garments grow heavy with their drink and pull her down to muddy death. Stepping calmly, regally, to the edge of the roof, mounting her golden throne. Slowly she takes the snake in her hand. The pull of immortal longings. Give me my robe, my crown. No more the juice of Egypt's grape shall moist these lips. Raises her fist coiled in venom. Presses the asp to her breast. Squeezes. To trigger the reptile's tiny brain into anger. To feel that sharp welcome pain like a lover's pinch. To cut the knot of her life. Finally to escape the crush of the ceiling, the trembling walls, she rushes down the alley, stumbling against the dead leaves and breaking a nail wrestling with the lock on the gate. She turns to look once more at the impassive façade of stones. The field sinking beneath her feet, the furrows like brown waves breaking into foam beneath the clouds of crows. Memories crowd her brain: her room, her father's face. The lights of the houses like fiery spheres in the fog, whirling, exploding among the snowy patches in the trees. Then, in an ecstasy of heroism, running down the hill, across the cowplank, the footpath, the alley, the market, to the pharmacy. I want it; give it to me. To kill the rats that keep her from sleeping. Against the wall in the laboratory, a key labelled

Capharnaüm. The third shelf, the blue jar, white powder. Don't ask me a single question. The bitter taste of ink in her mouth, the terrible thirst. Now, at last she hates no one. And after the vomiting blood, the convulsions, her whole body covered with spots, her pulse slipping like a stretched thread, like a harp string about to break, her hands wandering over the sheets as though to cover herself with the shroud, finally the priest and his oily thumb upon her eyes, her nostrils, her mouth, her hands and the soles of her feet. Too weak to hold the candle or the mirror. Her throat rattling in a room flooded with Latin syllables. And outside, the blind man's song: *In the heat of a summer's day a young girl dreams her heart away.* The third bell has rung. The shrill whistle of the train, the screech of the engine, clank of the chain. We were all created in order to be tormented and we know it; we only contrive to deceive ourselves. Why not put out the candle? There is nothing more to look at. She steps to the edge of the platform, the platform shaking, descends with a light rapid gait from the tower to the rails, close to the moving train, the bottom of the cars, linchpins, chains, the iron wheels of the front carriage, the ties covered in sand and coal dust. Measures the distance between the front and back wheels as they move past her, lets another car go by, hesitating the way one does before taking that first plunge into a cold stream, but keeping her eyes on the wheels of the approaching carriage. Now! She throws the red bag aside, draws her shoulders together, drops down under the carriage on her hands and rises again to her knees. A moment of doubt, *What am I doing?* and then the enormous, relentless weight knocking her back and dragging her by the shoulders. And the candle by which she had been reading flickers out. Climbing the stairs to the top of the house, long white candle flickering behind the shield of her hand. But the men are already in the house. She drops the candle, watches the flame catch the end of the curtains, the wall of fire rise up to protect her from the advancing men. And then the scorching heat becomes too much and she is outside on the battlements where it's cool and she can see them shouting and surrounding the house below. Behind her in the red sky, her whole life burning: she can see the old grandfather clock, the chandelier, the red carpet in the main hall of the castle, gold ferns and tree ferns, orchids and jasmine and the soft green velvet moss on the garden wall. *Qui est là? Qui est là?* Yes, she is standing on the battlements, her arms waving in the cool air and her hair streaming like flaming wings. There—a man climbing out of the skylight, coming toward her and calling *Bertha! Bertha!* The man, the fire, closing the distance. She yells and jumps, her hair streaming fire down to the pavement below.

The Queen, my Lord, is dead.

FC317.R458 1858 V.2

The crowd has finally crumbled under repeated police attacks and has been reduced to stragglers heading home, though their faces are still flushed with the optimism of riot. She walks aimlessly, unsure where to go. There's a hole where what just happened should be. All she knows is the patrols are out and about, teams on foot, blue paddywagons, motorcycle gangs. Also, her body feels vaguely sore, as though she's been beaten. She's lost her name, too, but that feeling is familiar. One thing she recognizes: the stench of tear gas on her clothes. She knows enough to keep moving, drifting along with pockets of mourners, if that's what they are. Walking as fast as she can without openly running. The dark streets, the dark sky, layer upon layer of dark clouds moving. Occasionally she can make out a pale haze where the moon should be. Without slowing her pace, she goes through a systematic self-frisk for clues. In the back pocket of her jeans (the only one still intact), she finds a crumpled card, a library card, the library card, muddied almost beyond recognition. An image flashes, or not really an image, at first it's just a sensation, the feel of a hand on her rump, and then a word: Clytæmnestra. Now she remembers. Clytæmnestra, beautiful Clytæmnestra. "I work alone," a hand slipping down her back, the pickpocket's skill, only in reverse, planting a library card. "Look out for yourself."

She stops running. Stands still, shaking slightly, in the current of dispersing demonstrators. She has forgotten her own name but she remembers Clytæmnestra and the rubber-kneed yearning she feels for her, all the more painful because it echoes in the empty arcade of her memory. Clytæmnestra is dead. She knows it, somehow. Or is this just the pain of unrequited love? What happened? Someone brushes past her, throwing her off balance, and she hears an approaching choir of motorcycles.

Keep moving. Vague recollections. Ché, a radio, that dandy little architect, tight little bow-tie and some crazy scheme, leafless trees, a muddy path, Rudy in drag, a pot on the fire, a knife. They're all gone. Wiped out. Only she and her riddled memory remain. And a library card. Which would be a place to go, to get off the street, if she knew where it was, in the meantime keep moving, head for the skyscrapers and the downtown area, rummage for clues, if only her head wasn't so completely empty except for Clytæmnestra, the knife, that's it, Clytæmnestra with the knife, surrounded by long nightsticks, murdered, gone down fighting. She knows it. Clytæmnestra's dead.

Running without thinking, crying, the snot running into her mouth, alone for the first time though she's always been alone, but feeling it for the first time, and angry, hating the pigs, herself because she screwed up, failed to stop her, to help, to go down with her, running anywhere, just running, turning the corner and smack into a foot patrol, which is like a slap in the face, waking her up, and her instincts, back the other way down a sidestreet, over a chain-link fence through an empty lot, watch out for the spring trash, bits of junk, broken glass, a syringe, slip through the gate under the chain and back out on the sidewalk, turn the corner and there it is, down the block, the cracked shell of the library, and emerging from the ruins, pausing under a bent lamppost, soaking wet and stinking to hell: that yellow dog.

Here at last, one that this one recognizes, yes, this is the hard, glabrous one that led the group up the slope of the mountain and into the forest, but moving fast now and full of a terror that this one can sense even though this one can barely snuffle anything through this one's own and thoroughly fecal stench, a fetidness which has persisted since this one emerged, not without enormous difficulty, from the place beneath the streets where the amaroidal ones, those hyperacidic brutes with long sticks, shoved this one and the First One after a long noxious voyage in the windowless vehicle, the terrible memory of that place beneath the street, the long tunnel, the terrible pungency invading this one's olfactory organ, a fetor that still refuses to release its grip, and then the sudden rush of water, the thick nidorous liquid pouring in through the tunnel all around them and rising, rising over their heads, the First One thrashing and choking alongside while this one struggles to stay afloat, and finally the broken grate, razor-sharp edges tearing at this one's flesh as this one pushes through to freedom, another tunnel and stone and brick and paper, broken books, twisted shelves, until finally this one can feel the cool air of the street, the dark night sky, a lamppost, safe but still full of the loss of the First One gone, drowned, and along with a premonitory pang of hunger, a heart racing in a kind of terror not unlike that of the one with the terete head now bent double and panting on the sidewalk beside this one who can at last, being once more in the company of the group, or at least having found one of the group, shake off some of the scum, even though the shaking, rather than re-establishing the bond between them, seems to have a contrary effect on the hairless one, but no time anyway for reunions because here's another van full of sticks and acidulous ones, so best they absquatulate back into the place full of old books and bricks, from which, just barely filtering through the fruitiness of this one's sewage-soaked fur, there's a faint trace of mildew.

She hesitates between the threat of the paddywagon and the awful stink of the dog, but then his name comes to her and she follows Pilote into the ruins of the library. The card turns out to be unnecessary; the staff has abandoned ship. So that's it then, they're alone, just her and this sewer mutt. In a way, she's glad of his company. If he didn't stink so totally badly, she'd be tempted to hug or pet him or whatever one does with a dog. Although, if he shakes himself again, she'll have to kill him. Inside, the random collapse of walls and shelves has transformed the already arcane system of the library into an unreadable maze. Still, she feels safe in here. The stillness among the toppled corridors of old books and, when she gets enough rows between her and Pilote, the musty smell, the smell of time. What is she looking for? A clue? Something to fill the gaps in her memory? Or just a place to hide from the homeless patrols? The air is perfectly still, the stink of Pilote competing with the decay of knowledge. If she stays in here long enough, or winds deeply down the staircases into the belly of the building, the pain of Clytæmnestra might somehow be shut out or worn down or made bearable. Finally, she runs out of running and stops beside a shelf of leather-bound antique volumes. As soon as she stops, a wave of exhaustion washes over her; she feels, suddenly, the pain in all her muscles, her wrung-out lungs, her pumping heart, and she has to sit down on the floor.

Pilote settles down too close beside her and begins sawing a canine tooth on the edge of a hardcover. He's probably famished. For the first time since she entered the building, it occurs to her that these are actually books all around her and she might look more closely at them. This is her first time in a library, unless it isn't but she's forgotten. She leans past Pilote and pulls the large volume he's been gnawing on closer. The dog turns a wet resentful eye on her, drags himself onto his feet and moves a few yards away. The book is very old—half the spine crumbles in her hand when she opens it—full of scrolled letters and ancient French. Still, she can make out the title, *Relations*, that it was written by Jesuits and that they are talking about her city. This is a surprise. There are thousands of books here. Yet the first one she's opened has, in some way, touched her. Is it coincidence? A strange thrill runs faintly through her, a kind of excitement, like finding a fresh stack of garbage bags in the alley behind Joe's Steak House and no one else around to take your prize from you. At first, you don't know where to start. She moves, on all fours, down the row a little way to pick another volume at random. As she draws the text from its place on the shelf, she glimpses Pilote through the emptied slot. He's busily chewing on what at first she assumes to be another book. But something catches her eye, a glint of white like bone. Pilote, as though he senses her eyes on him, turns and raises his head to look back at her, his eyes shining, his snout red with blood.

fin

Notes

7 "¡Qué esfuerzo… ser perro!" [How hard the horse tries to be a dog!]:
Federico García Lorca, "Death" in *Poet in New York*, translated by Greg
Simon and Steven F. White (New York: Farrar, Straus and Giroux, 1988).

7 "ἆρ᾽ ἐστί σοι ὀβολὸς περισσός ;" [Have you an obol to spare?]:
my thanks to Gabriel Baugniet for the ancient Greek.

16 "Rien à faire": Samuel Beckett, *Waiting for Godot*, act i, scene i.

17 "A ce soldat brisé… le loup flaire!"
[This broken soldier! Must he then despair
Of having cross and tomb,
This dying man the wolf already sniffs!]:
Charles Baudelaire, "The Irreparable" in *The Flowers of Evil*, translated by
James McGowan (Oxford and New York: Oxford University Press, 1993).

17 "The duty of a revolutionary is to make revolution": Ernesto Guevara, cited
in Daniel James, *Ché Guevara: A Biography* (New York: Stein and Day, 1969),
p. 302.

18 "We must carry the war… within his barracks": Guevara, "Message to the
Tricontinental" in *Ché: Selected Works of Ernesto Guevara*, edited by Rolando
E. Bonachea and Nelson P. Valdes (Cambridge, Mass. and London:
The MIT Press, 1969), p. 180.

18 "Into the streets with poems and guns": Pablo Neruda, "Letter to Miguel
Otero Silva, in Caracas (1948)" in *Neruda and Vallejo: Selected Poems*,
translated by Robert Bly (Boston: Beacon Press, 1971).

19 "You will have time… leisure": Lorca, "The Old Lizard," translated by
Lysander Kemp in *The Selected Poems*, edited by Francisco García Lorca
and Donald M. Allen (New York: New Directions, 1955).

19 "Blow wind!… on our back": William Shakespeare, *Macbeth*, act v, scene v.

19 "Hand me the man-axe, someone, hurry!": Æschylus, *The Libation Bearers*,
translated by Robert Fagles, 876.

19 "Fie my lord…": *Macbeth*, act v, scene i.

23 "The fountain pen, the briar pipe…Decoration is disease and crime": this is a combination of excerpts from Le Corbusier's *L'Art décoratif d'aujourd'hui* and *La Peinture moderne* as cited in Charles Jencks, *Le Corbusier and the Tragic View of Architecture* (Cambridge: Harvard University Press, 1973).

27 "The city is the crack of the whip…The city designed Le Corbusier": from a letter cited in Jencks, *Le Corbusier and the Tragic View*, p. 23.

27 "Black with soot…moral degradation": author's translation of Le Corbusier, *Quand les cathédrales étaient blanches* (Paris: Gonthier, 1965), pp. 12–13.

34 "Who would have thought…" and other phrases in this passage are from various scenes in *Macbeth*.

39 "Messieurs…en autant d'Iroquois": sieur de Maisonneuve, cited in Robert Rumilly, *Histoire de Montréal*, vol. 1 (Montreal: Fides, 1970), p. 38.

42 "on the terrace, wrestling with the moon": Lorca, "Dance of Death" in *Poet in New York.*

43 "the Divine Watchmakers' Trust": Julio Cortázar, *Hopscotch*, translated by Gregory Rabassa (New York: Random House, 1966), p. 372.

46 "We need two, three Vietnams": Guevara, cited in James, *Ché Guevara*, p. 275.

51 "Hatred growing…and silence": Neruda, "Dictators" in *Neruda and Vallejo.*

55 "Don't shoot…than dead": Ché's words at the moment of his capture in Bolivia, cited in James, *Ché Guevara,* p. 14.

57 "the river were remembering…its drowned": Lorca, "Fable and Round of the Three Friends," translated by Ben Belitt in *Selected Poems.*

59 "a vast limitless plain…within the mind": based on Le Corbusier, cited by Norma Evenson in "Le Corbusier: The Machine and the Grand Design" (1969), reprinted in *Modern Arts Criticism*, vol. 3 (Detroit: Gale Research, 1991), p. 303.

60 "Once Rome ruled…is beauty": based on Le Corbusier, *Vers une architecture* (1923), cited by Charles Jencks in "Le Corbusier" in *Modern Arts Criticism*, vol. 3, p. 307.

62 "the grinding bad luck…hands shaking": Neruda, "The Heights of Macchu Picchu: III" in *Neruda and Vallejo.*

65 "Real heroes…not a casualty": Le Corbusier, cited in Jencks, *Le Corbusier and the Tragic View*, p. 59.

68 "The Parthenon, that terrifying machine!...reduced to dust": based on Le Corbusier, *Le Voyage d'Orient* (1966), cited in Jencks, *Le Corbusier and the Tragic View*, p. 34.

69 "The spirit of the Parthenon...Modulor is the secret": based on Le Corbusier, *Le Modulor: Contre la pollution visuelle* (Paris: Denoël/Gonthier, 1977), p. 54.

72 "Mermelade y Sangre": Neruda, "Sexual Water" in *Neruda and Vallejo.*

73 "As he placed the weight...of the desert": Pierre Benoit, *Maisonneuve* (Tours, France: MAME, 1960), author's translation, p. 48.

74 "Kontírio...and lakes" and other Mohawk phrases and their translations are based on the "Mohawk Opening Prayer" as cited in Paul A. Wallace, *The White Roots of Peace* (New York: Chauncy Press, 1985); "Prière d'ouverture Mohawk" and "L'enseignement du clan" in *Pleine Terre: Visions Autochtones*, vol. 2, no. 1, (June 1993); and *Ohen:ton Kariwentehkwen* (Kahnawake, Quebec: Kanien'kéha Owén:na Otióhkwa/Mohawk Language Curriculum Centre, n.d.).

74 "the moon and a serpent...seven sins": based on Baudelaire, "To a Madonna" in *The Flowers of Evil.*

81 "The sun drowning in its own blood": based on Baudelaire, "The Harmony of Evening" in *The Flowers of Evil.*

82 "What matters...River's mouth": Lorca, "Christmas on the Hudson" in *Poet in New York.*

82 "It was a matter of occupying...sun-scorched fields": Le Corbusier, cited by Evenson in *Modern Arts Criticism*, vol. 3, p. 303.

82 "O, Mother of Roman games and Greek delights": Baudelaire, "Lesbos" in *The Flowers of Evil.*

82 "Tell my wife that she should remarry": Ché Guevara's last words to his executioner, cited in James, *Ché Guevara*, p. 17.

82 "O, Whale of all the skies": Lorca, "The Poet Prays to the Virgin for Help," cited in his own "Lecture: A Poet in New York," translated by Christopher Maurer in *Poet in New York.*

83 "breathe the perfume...asleep in my hands": based on Baudelaire, "Beside a Monstrous Jewish Whore," "The Balcony," "The Possessed," "To One Who Is Too Cheerful," and "Lethe" in *The Flowers of Evil.*

87 "Teiethinonhwera:ton...our Mother" and other italicized phrases: excerpts from *Ohen:ton Kariwentehkwen.*

91 "Je leur ai dit…à moi": Le Corbusier, cited in *Le Corbusier: le passé à réaction poétique* (Paris: Caisse nationale de monuments historiques et des sites/Ministère de la culture et de la communication, 1988), p. 34.

92 "Mathematics…the land of numbers": Le Corbusier, *Le Modulor*, p. 71.

93 The letter is based on Guevara's "Letter to Fidel" in *Selected Works*, pp. 422–423.

94 "Let's Beat Up the Poor": Baudelaire, in *Twenty Prose Poems*, translated by Michael Hamburger (San Francisco: City Lights Books, 1988).

94 "Balboa, your dog…unknown forest": Neruda, "The Head on the Pole" in *Neruda and Vallejo*.

94 "November 7…of this region": from Guevara's Bolivian diary, cited in James, *Ché Guevara*, p. 214.

96 "who doubts my manhood…personal contest": Rudolph Valentino, "Letter to the Editor of the Chicago Tribune," cited in Alan Arnold, *Valentino* (London: Hutchinson, 1952).

98 "To take possession…in time": Le Corbusier, *Le Modulor*, p. 28.

98 "Man walks in a straight line…he goes straight to it": Le Corbusier, cited in Jencks, *Le Corbusier and the Tragic View*, p. 70.

98 "Modulor is anthropocentric…miracle of numbers": this passage and ensuing dialogue by Le Corbusier based on Le Corbusier, *Le Modulor*.

103 "When the pure forms…murdered me": Lorca, "Fable and Round of the Three Friends," translated by Belitt in *Selected Poems*.

106 "Ce que vous voyez…un grand arbre": Rumilly, *Histoire de Montréal*, p. 159.

111 "The correct handling…with the enemy": Mao Zedong, "On the Correct Handling of Contradictions Among the People" in *Selected Works of Mao Tsetung* (Mao Zedong), vol. 5 (Beijing: Foreign Language Press, 1977), p. 384.

112 "A heart abyssal…Æschylus's dream": Baudelaire, "The Ideal" in *The Flowers of Evil*.

114 "Caminito que el…viste pasar" [Little path erased by time, one day you saw us pass]: from *Caminito*, lyrics by Gabino Coria Peñaloza, music by Juan de Dios Filiberto.

114 "A fetter…": here and throughout the section, passages from Karl Marx, *Das Kapital*, translated by S. Moore and E. Aveling (Moscow: Foreign Language Publishing House, 1954).

114   "he venido…mi mal" [I have come one last time, I have come to tell you my pain]: *Caminito.*

114   "Caminito…en flor" [Small path that was once bordered with clover and flowering jute]: *Caminito.*

115   "una sombra ya pronto serás" [soon you'll be no more than a shade…]: *Caminito.*

115   "Bloody, bold…of men": *Macbeth*, act iv, scene i.

115   "For none of woman born…Macbeth": *Macbeth,* act iv, scene i.

115   "una sombra, lo mismo que yo" [a shade, just like me]: *Caminito.*

115   "A child, yellow curls in a jewelled crown": *Macbeth*, act iv, scene i.

116   "And a widow's vengeful…winds of Thrace": Æschylus, *Agamemnon*, translated by Robert Fagles, 1441–1444.

117   "Ah, remorse…poisoned shafts": Baudelaire, "The Irreparable" in *The Flowers of Evil.*

117   "Remorse is the worm that will eat your flesh": Baudelaire, "Remorse After Death" in *The Flowers of Evil.*

117   "a sad thought dancing": based on Rudolph Valentino, "The tango is a sad thought that is danced," quoted in Arnold, *Valentino.*

117   "Broken hearts…black city": Baudelaire, "Lethe" and "Mœsta et errabunda" in *The Flowers of Evil.*

118   "…te juré…también"
[I swore my love for you
was greater than my love for my own soul
or for my own mother]:
from *Recordandote,* lyrics by G.D. Barbieri, music by J. de Grandis.

118   "Te acoplaste…colvió"
[You slept with any bum
from the lowest slum
and I swear any lousy teamster
could have you at will]:
Recordandote.

118   "Do not draw…jealous God": *Agamemnon*, 914.

118   "Wash your hands…on's grave": *Macbeth*, act v, scene i.

118   "Come. A great victor…royal road": *Agamemnon*, 936.

118 "Se acabaron…corazón"
[This is an end to verses
from my pilgrim's inspiration
since the most divine of verses
was to hold you in my heart]:
Recordandote.

119 "The moon dancing…the Dead": Lorca, "Dance of the Moon in Santiago,"
translated by Norman di Giovanni in *Selected Poems.*

119 "Struck deep…deep": *Agamemnon*, 1368.

119 "Pensé que…causó"
[Of all the verses of my life,
I thought you were the most intense,
because this wound still bleeds
which your cheating has inflicted]:
Recordandote.

119 "So he goes down…ripped her into birth": based on *Agamemnon*, 1410–1415.

119 "for the smoke of hell…*Hold, hold!*" *Macbeth*, act i, scene v.

119 "Endless words…is steel": *Agamemnon*, 1391–1400.

120 "Ya que…pasión"
[Now that you know the secret
of the degree of my suffering,
tell me who could have wanted you
with a greater passion]:
Recordandote.

120 "Life is neither noble, nor good, nor sacred": Lorca, "Ode to Walt Whitman,"
translated by Stephen Spender and J.L. Gili in *Selected Poems.*

121 "Keeping watch…arms of stone": Neruda, "Sonata and Destructions" in
Neruda and Vallejo.

121 "the inkwell of the city spills into the river": Lorca, "The Martyrdom of
Saint Eulalia" in *Selected Poems.*

121 "heart takes flight from the black city": Baudelaire, "Mœsta et errabunda" in
The Flowers of Evil.

123 "There was an occupation…never is": Gertrude Stein, "Portrait of Mabel
Dodge at the Villa Curonia" in *Selected Writings of Gertrude Stein* (New York:
Random House, 1946).

123 "There is that caressing…that caressing": Stein, "Tender Buttons" in *Selected Writings*.

133 "A new public ballroom…well-run" and subsequent quotes are from *The Chicago Tribune* (July 19, 1926), cited in Brad Steiger and Chaw Mank, *Valentino* (London: Corgi Books, 1976).

133 "To the austerity…permit it": Guevara, cited in James, *Ché Guevara*, p. 315.

133 "It so happens I am sick of being a man": Neruda, "Walking Around" in *Neruda and Vallejo*.

137 "Hwe-do-ne-e-e-eh?" [When will this come to pass?]: "Constitution of the Five Nations" in Arthur C. Parker, *Parker on the Iroquois*, edited by William N. Fenton (Syracuse, N.Y.: Syracuse University Press, 1968).

137 "a line of crosses rocking": based on Lorca, "Poem of the Saeta," translated by Jaime de Angulo in *Selected Poems*.

137 "two small threads of blood splitting the hard sky": Lorca, "The Birth of Christ" in *Poet in New York*.

137 "Let the earth…kneeling in the snow": *The Jesuit Relations and Allied Documents*, vol. 48, edited R.G. Thwaites, translated by F. Alexander, P.F. Bicknell, C. Lindsay and W. Price (New York: Pageant Book Company, 1959), pp. 41–45.

139 "like shipwrecked survivors": based on Lorca, "Through the suburbs sleepless people stagger, / as though just delivered from a shipwreck of blood" from "The Dawn" in *Poet in New York*.

140 "a broken soldier": Baudelaire, "The Irreparable" in *The Flowers of Evil*.

145 "an empty shoe…no dogs": Neruda, "Nothing but Death" in *Neruda and Vallejo*.

147 "A vague astronomy of shapeless pistols": Lorca, "Ballad of the Spanish Civil Guard," translated by A.L. Lloyd in *Selected Poems*.

147 "Arm, arm…no tarrying here": *Macbeth*, act v, scene v.

150 "wave upon wave…strange sounds": Rudolph Valentino, on his arrival in New York City, cited in Arnold, *Valentino*.

150 "Threaten away!…the throne is yours": *Agamemnon*, 1448–1451.

150 "leaden skulls": Lorca, "Ballad of the Spanish Civil Guard" in *Selected Poems*.

151 "Come, Orestes…hunt you down": Æschylus, *The Libation Bearers*, 911.

152 "tired of the world": *Macbeth*, act v, scene v.

152 "O happy dagger...let me die": Shakespeare, *Romeo and Juliet*, act v, scene iii.

153 "She's standing...pinks filling the air": adapted from Kate Chopin, *The Awakening* (New York: Penguin, 1984), p. 176.

153 "Rosemary for remembrance...and violets": Shakespeare, *Hamlet*, act iv, scene vi.

153 "And now your sister's drowned...to muddy death": *Hamlet*, act iv, scene vii.

153 "The pull of immortal...the knot of her life": Shakespeare, *Antony and Cleopatra*, act v, scene ii.

153 "Finally to escape...*dreams her heart away*": adapted from Gustave Flaubert, *Madame Bovary*, translated by Paul de Man (New York and London: W.W. Norton, 1965), pp. 228–238.

154 "The third bell...dragging her by the shoulders": adapted from Leo Tolstoy, *Anna Karenina*, vol. 2, translated by Rachelle S. Townsend (London: J.M. Dent & Sons, 1958), pp. 314–316.

154 "And the candle...to the pavement below": adapted from Charlotte Brontë, *Jane Eyre* (London: J.M. Dent & Sons, 1908), pp. 431–432 and Jean Rhys, *Wide Sargasso Sea* (London: Andre Deutsch, 1966), pp. 188–190.

155 "The Queen, my Lord, is dead": *Macbeth*, act v, scene v.